Plants vs. Zombies

RUMBLE AT LAKE GUMBO #3

ABDO
Spotlight

DARK HORSE BOOKS

PopCap

Written by **PAUL TOBIN**

Art by **RON CHAN**

Colors by **MATT J. RAINWATER**

Letters by **STEVE DUTRO**

Cover by **RON CHAN**

"Zomboss' Fashionable Beach Wear!"
Bonus Paper Doll Kit by
CHRISTIANNE GILLENARDO-GOUDREAU

"Tales of Stirring Romance"
Bonus Story by
KEVIN BURKHALTER

President and Publisher **MIKE RICHARDSON**
Editor **PHILIP R. SIMON**
Assistant Editor **MEGAN WALKER**
Designer **BRENNAN THOME**
Digital Art Technician **CHRISTINA McKENZIE**

Special thanks to Alexandria Land, A.J. Rathbun, Kristen Star, and everyone at PopCap Games.

DarkHorse.com
PopCap.com

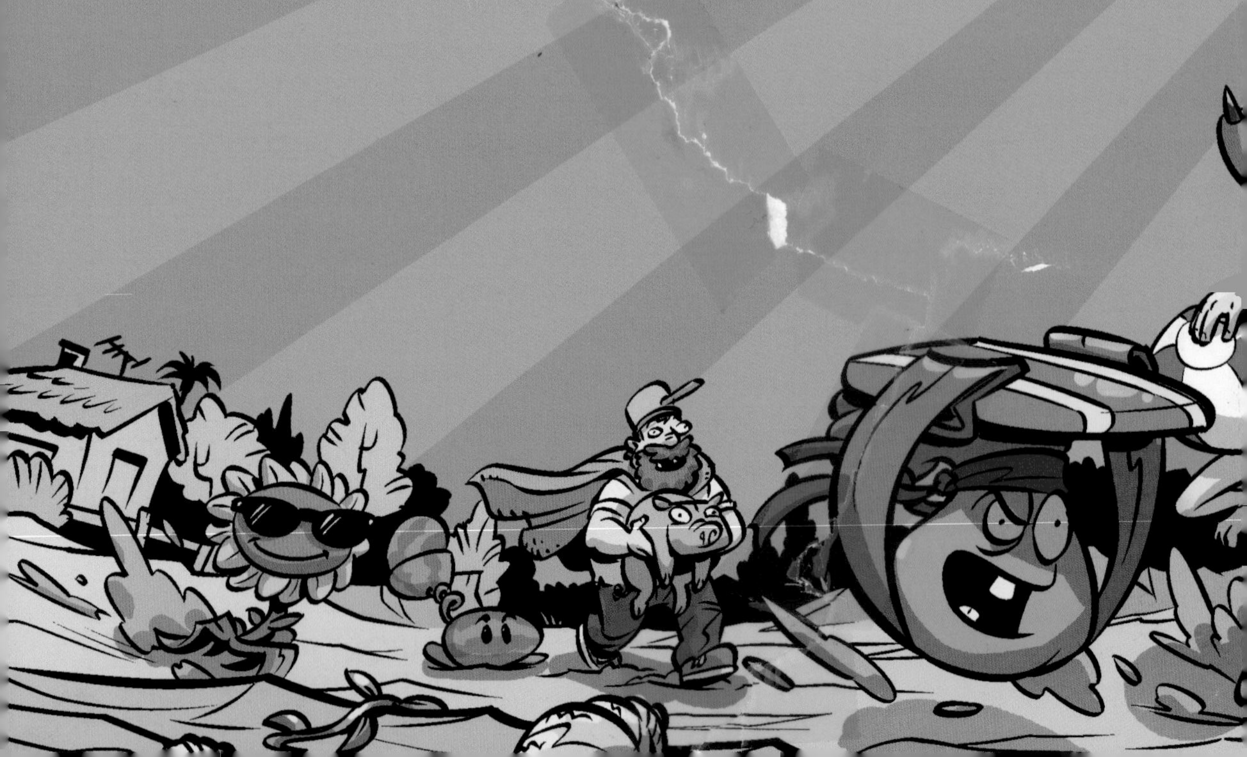

PLANTS VS. ZOMBIES™

RUMBLE AT LAKE GUMBO #3

ABDOBOOKS.COM

Reinforced library bound edition published in 2021 by Spotlight, a division of ABDO, PO Box 398166, Minneapolis, Minnesota 55439. Spotlight produces high-quality reinforced library bound editions for schools and libraries.
Published by agreement with Dark Horse Comics.

Printed in the United States of America, North Mankato, Minnesota.
092020
012021

THIS BOOK CONTAINS RECYCLED MATERIALS

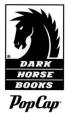

Library of Congress Control Number: 2020940824

Publisher's Cataloging-in-Publication Data

Names: Tobin, Paul, author. | Chan, Ron, illustrator.
Title: Rumble at Lake Gumbo / writer: Paul Tobin; art: Ron Chan.
Description: Minneapolis, Minnesota: Spotlight, 2021 | Series: Plants vs. zombies
Summary: Patrice and Nate must defend Lake Gumbo from another zombie invasion when Dr. Zomboss attempts to pollute the lake.
Identifiers: ISBN 9781532147630 (#1; lib. bdg.) | ISBN 9781532147647 (#2; lib. bdg.) | ISBN 9781532147654 (#3; lib. bdg.)
Subjects: LCSH: Plants vs. zombies (Game)--Juvenile fiction. | Plants--Juvenile fiction. | Zombies--Juvenile fiction. | Lakes--Juvenile fiction. | Pollution--Juvenile fiction. | Graphic novels--Juvenile fiction. | Comic books, strips, etc.--Juvenile fiction.
Classification: DDC 741.5--dc23

Spotlight

A Division of ABDO
abdobooks.com

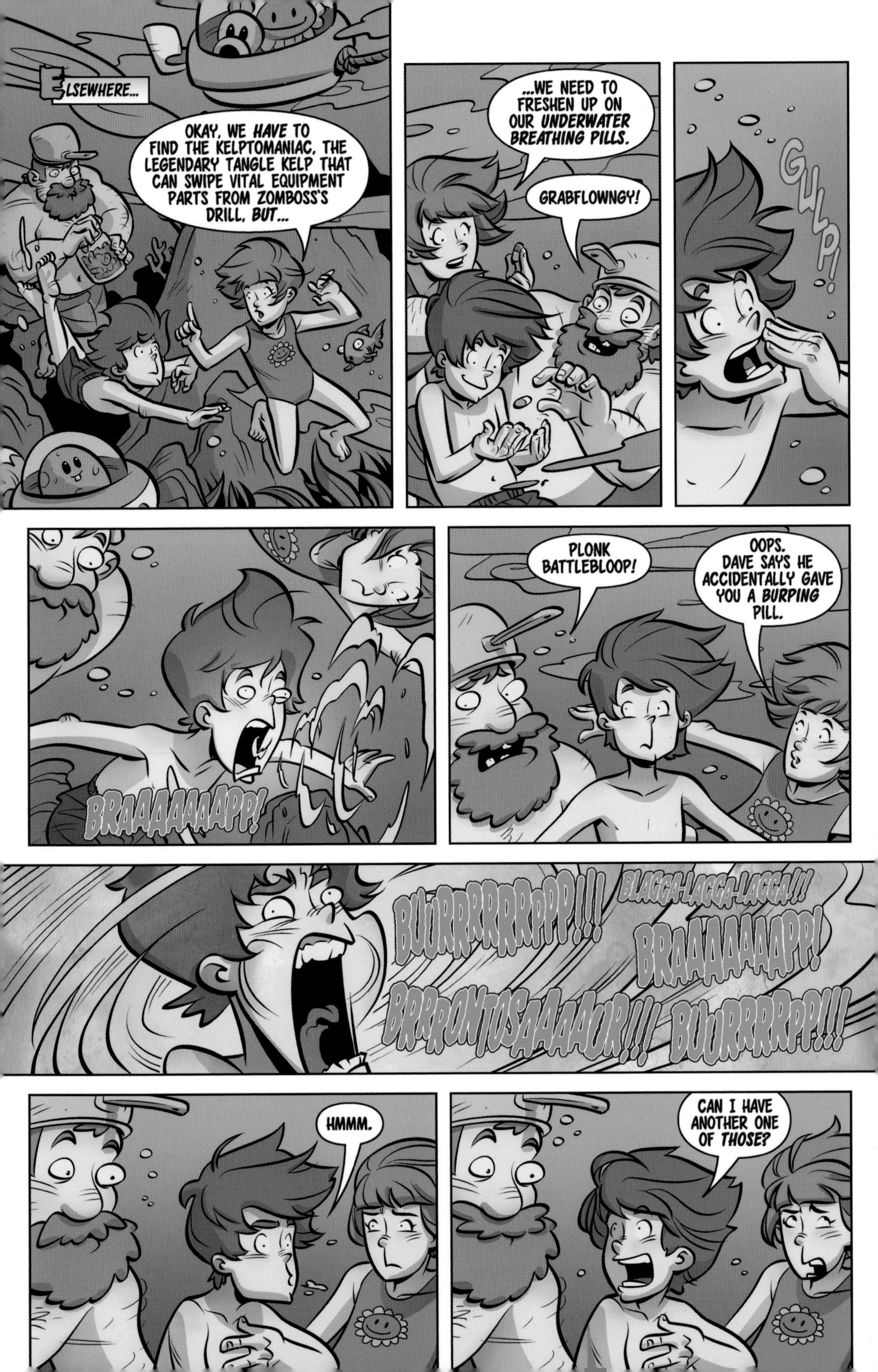
ELSEWHERE...
OKAY, WE HAVE TO FIND THE KELPTOMANIAC, THE LEGENDARY TANGLE KELP THAT CAN SWIPE VITAL EQUIPMENT PARTS FROM ZOMBOSS'S DRILL, BUT...
...WE NEED TO FRESHEN UP ON OUR UNDERWATER BREATHING PILLS.
GRABFLOWNGY!
GULP!
BRAAAAAAAPP!
PLONK BATTLEBLOOP!
OOPS. DAVE SAYS HE ACCIDENTALLY GAVE YOU A BURPING PILL.
BUURRRRRRPPP!!!
BLAGGA-LAGGA-LAGGA!!
BRAAAAAAAPP!
BRRRONTOSAAAAUR!!!
BUURRRRPP!!!
HMMM.
CAN I HAVE ANOTHER ONE OF THOSE?

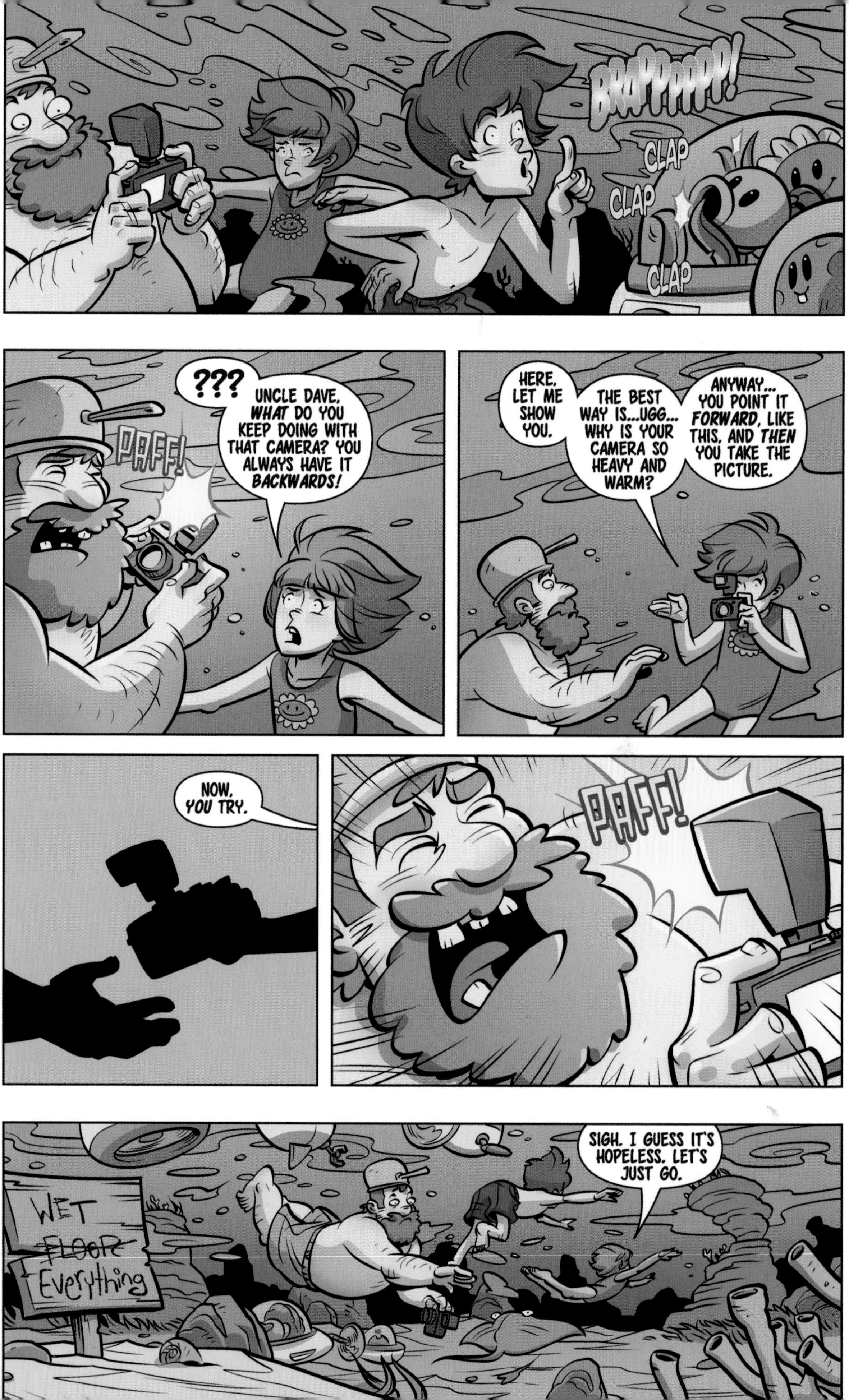
BRAPPPPPP!
CLAP
CLAP
CLAP
???
UNCLE DAVE, WHAT DO YOU KEEP DOING WITH THAT CAMERA? YOU ALWAYS HAVE IT BACKWARDS!
PAFF!
HERE, LET ME SHOW YOU.
THE BEST WAY IS...UGG... WHY IS YOUR CAMERA SO HEAVY AND WARM?
ANYWAY... YOU POINT IT FORWARD, LIKE THIS, AND THEN YOU TAKE THE PICTURE.
NOW, YOU TRY.
PAFF!
SIGH. I GUESS IT'S HOPELESS. LET'S JUST GO.
WET FLOOR Everything

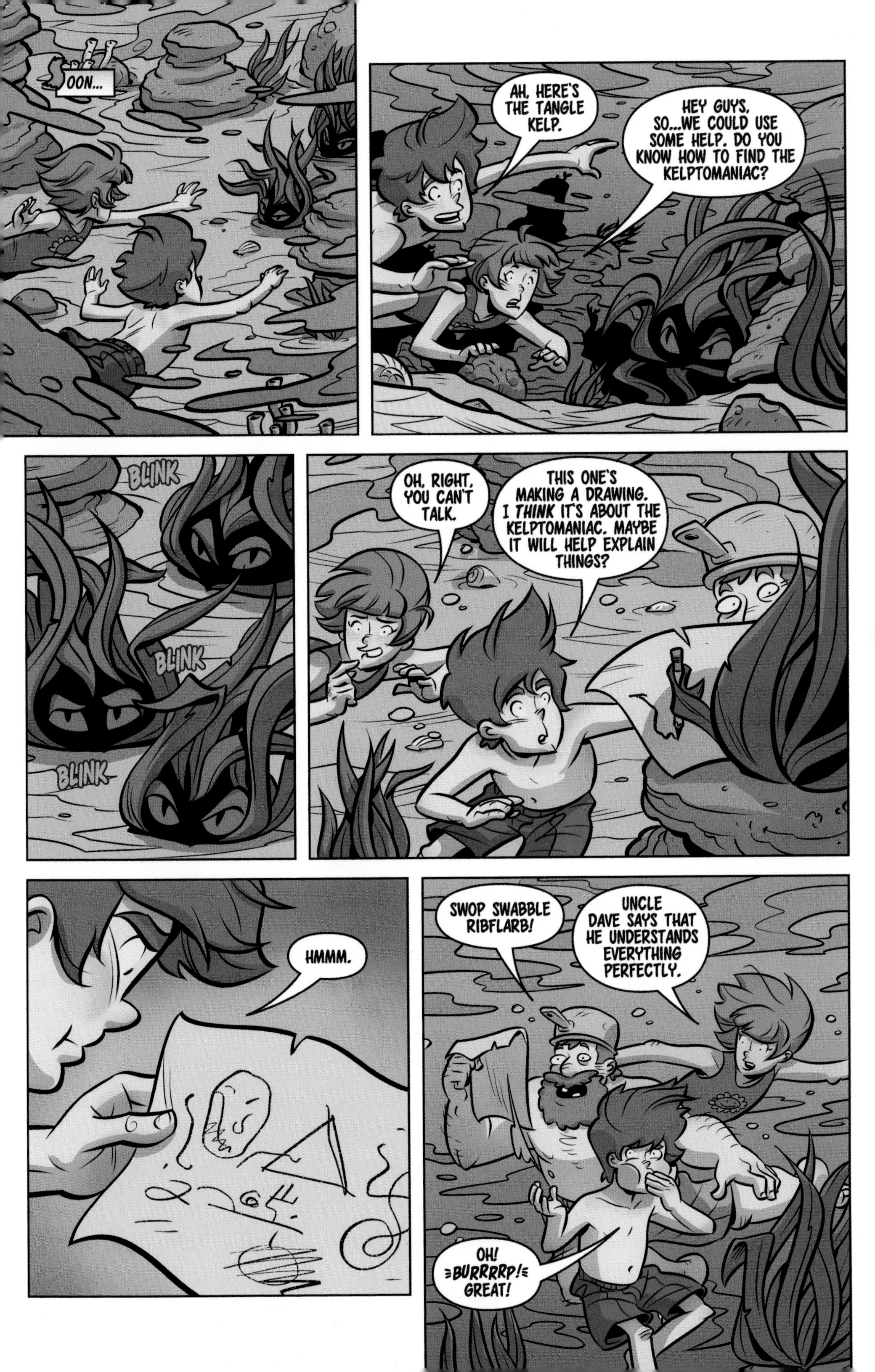

OON...
AH, HERE'S THE TANGLE KELP.
HEY GUYS, SO...WE COULD USE SOME HELP. DO YOU KNOW HOW TO FIND THE KELPTOMANIAC?
BLINK
BLINK
BLINK
OH, RIGHT, YOU CAN'T TALK.
THIS ONE'S MAKING A DRAWING. I *THINK* IT'S ABOUT THE KELPTOMANIAC. MAYBE IT WILL HELP EXPLAIN THINGS?
HMMM.
SWOP SWABBLE RIBFLARB!
UNCLE DAVE SAYS THAT HE UNDERSTANDS EVERYTHING PERFECTLY.
OH! *BURRRRP!* GREAT!

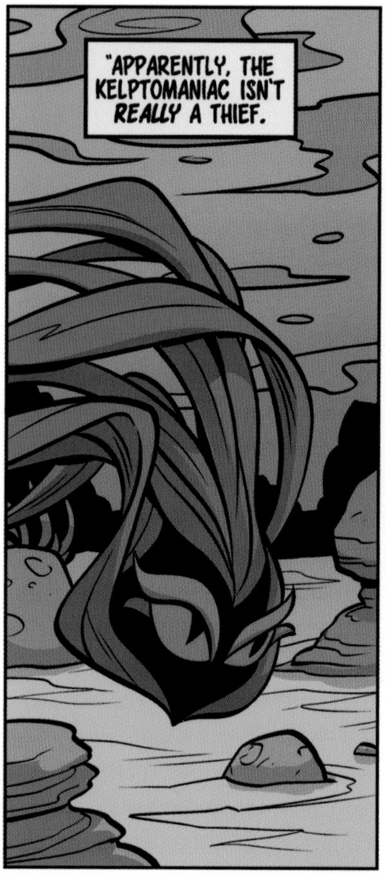
"APPARENTLY, THE KELPTOMANIAC ISN'T *REALLY* A THIEF.

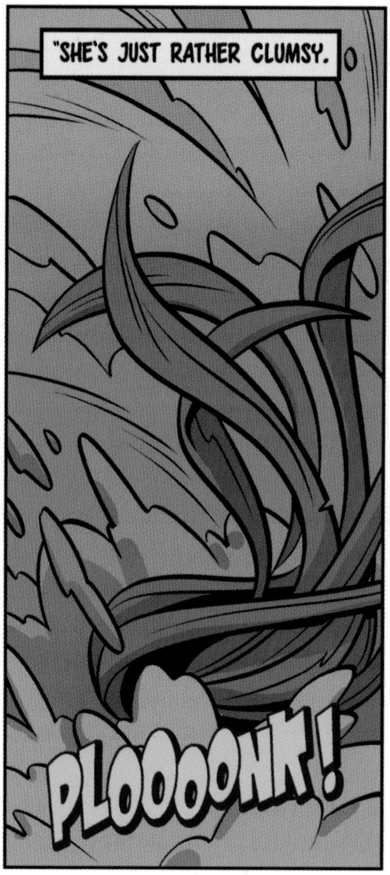
"SHE'S JUST RATHER CLUMSY.
PLOOOONK!

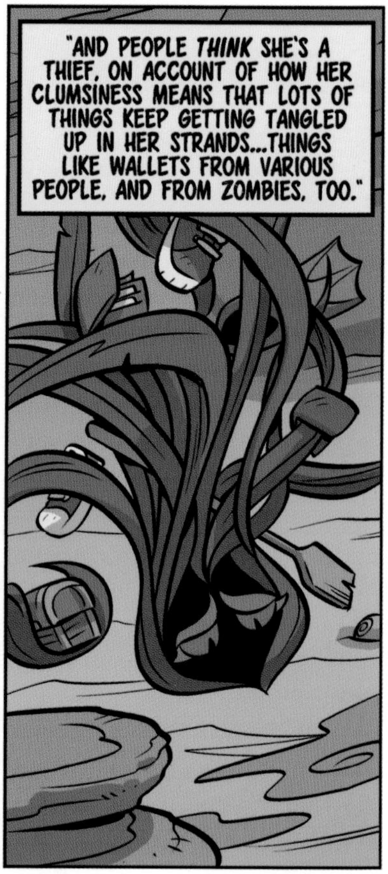
"AND PEOPLE *THINK* SHE'S A THIEF, ON ACCOUNT OF HOW HER CLUMSINESS MEANS THAT LOTS OF THINGS KEEP GETTING TANGLED UP IN HER STRANDS...THINGS LIKE WALLETS FROM VARIOUS PEOPLE, AND FROM ZOMBIES, TOO."

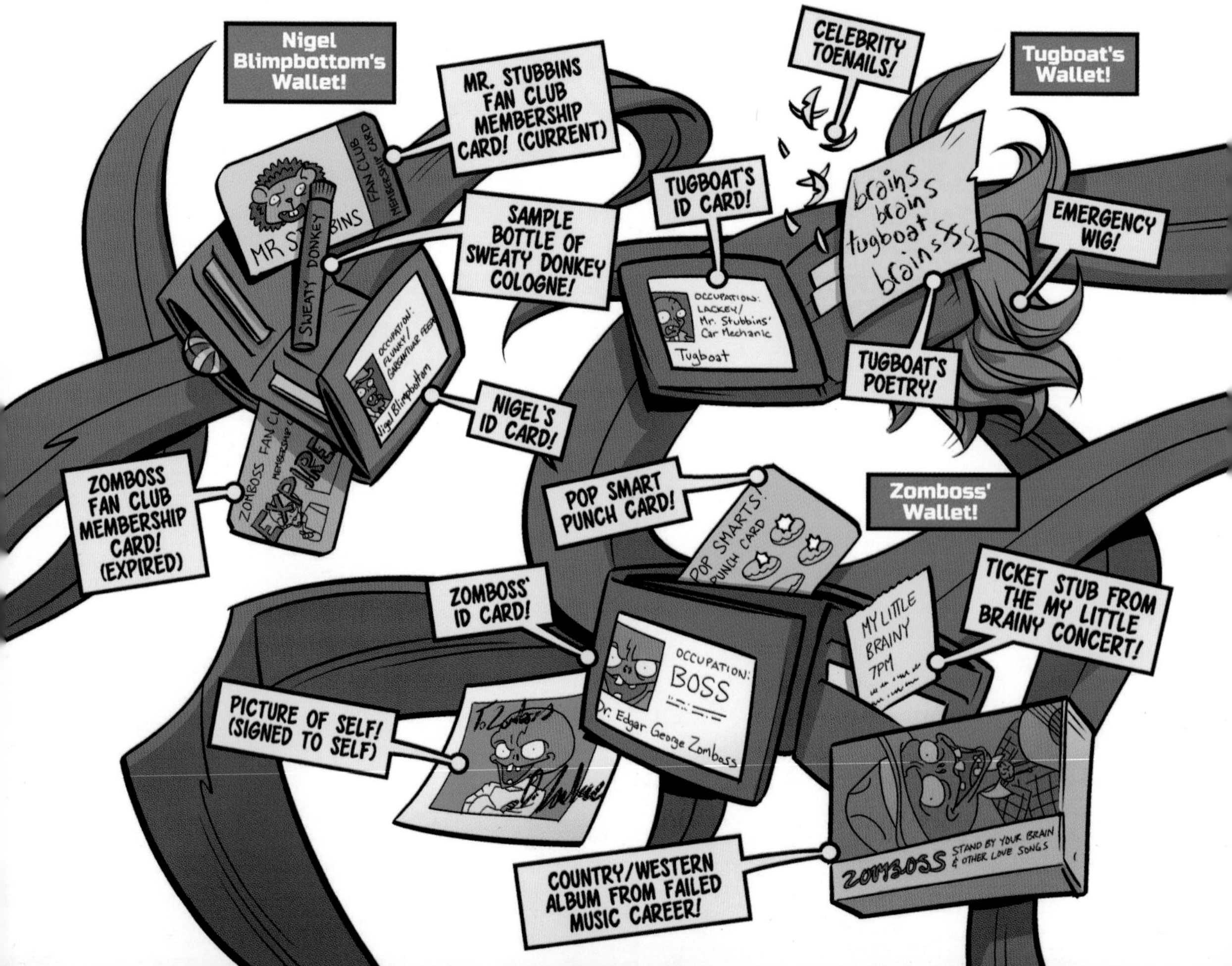
Nigel Blimpbottom's Wallet!
MR. STUBBINS FAN CLUB MEMBERSHIP CARD! (CURRENT)
FAN CLUB
MEMBERSHIP CARD
MR STUBBINS
SAMPLE BOTTLE OF SWEATY DONKEY COLOGNE!
SWEATY DONKEY
NIGEL'S ID CARD!
Nigel Blimpbottom
ZOMBOSS FAN CLUB MEMBERSHIP CARD! (EXPIRED)
ZOMBOSS FAN CLUB
MEMBERSHIP
EXPIRED
CELEBRITY TOENAILS!
Tugboat's Wallet!
TUGBOAT'S ID CARD!
OCCUPATIONS: LACKEY/ Mr. Stubbins' Car Mechanic
Tugboat
brains brains tugboat brainsssss
EMERGENCY WIG!
TUGBOAT'S POETRY!
POP SMART PUNCH CARD!
POP SMARTS! PUNCH CARD
Zomboss' Wallet!
ZOMBOSS' ID CARD!
OCCUPATION: BOSS
Dr. Edgar George Zomboss
TICKET STUB FROM THE MY LITTLE BRAINY CONCERT!
MY LITTLE BRAINY 7PM
PICTURE OF SELF! (SIGNED TO SELF)
COUNTRY/WESTERN ALBUM FROM FAILED MUSIC CAREER!
ZOMBOSS
STAND BY YOUR BRAIN & OTHER LOVE SONGS

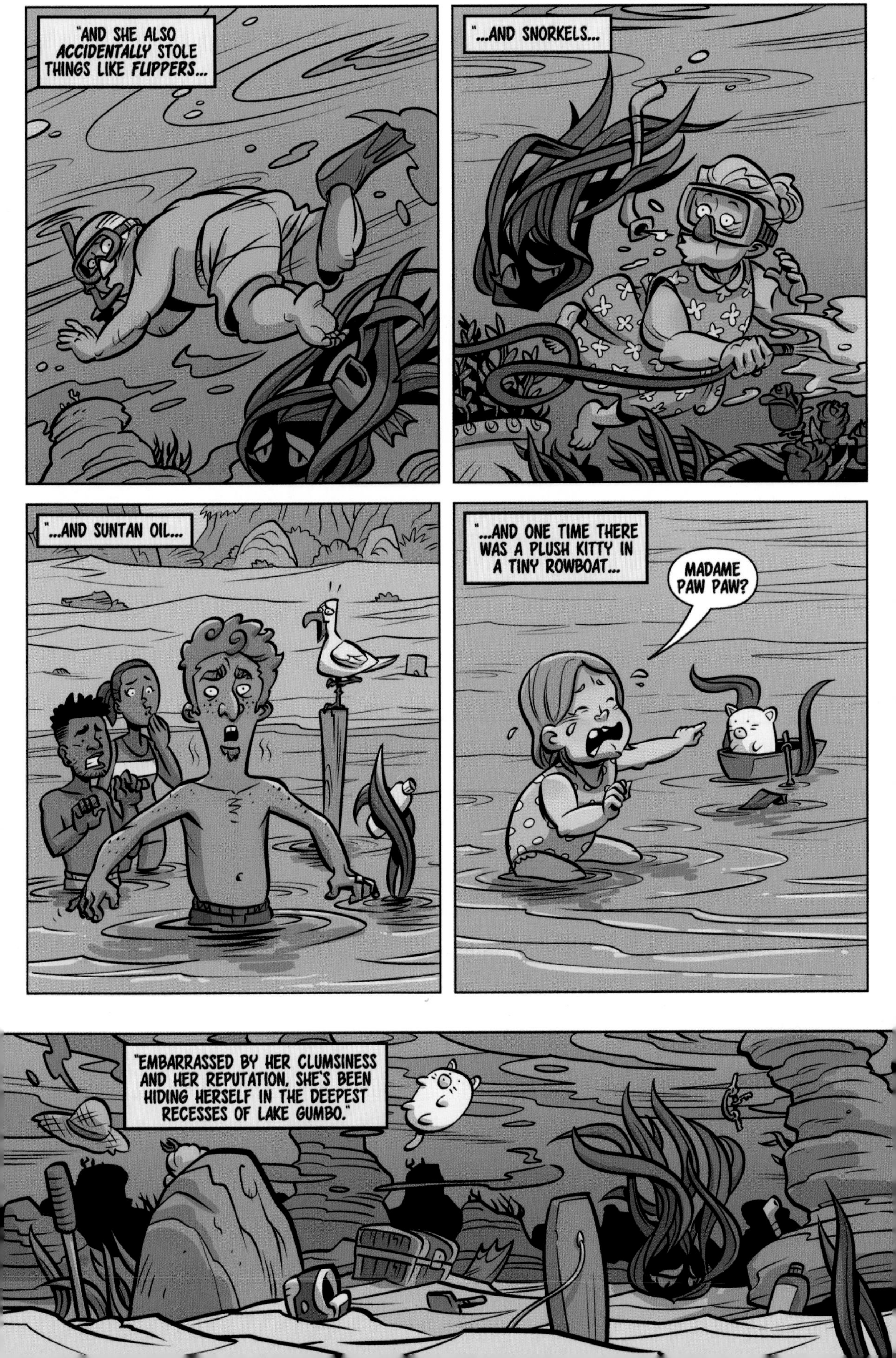
"AND SHE ALSO ACCIDENTALLY STOLE THINGS LIKE FLIPPERS...
"...AND SNORKELS...
"...AND SUNTAN OIL...
"...AND ONE TIME THERE WAS A PLUSH KITTY IN A TINY ROWBOAT...
MADAME PAW PAW?
"EMBARRASSED BY HER CLUMSINESS AND HER REPUTATION, SHE'S BEEN HIDING HERSELF IN THE DEEPEST RECESSES OF LAKE GUMBO."

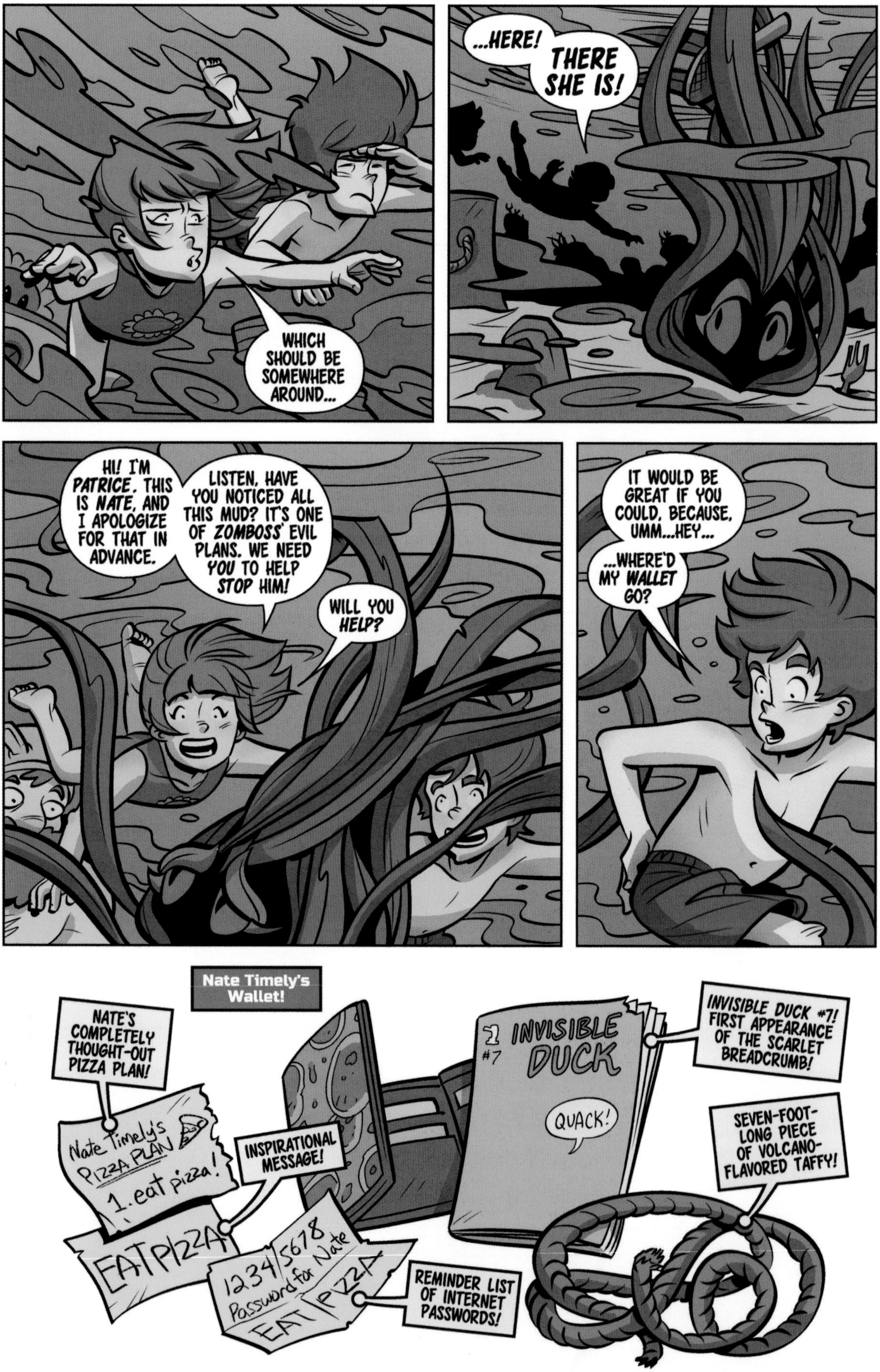

WHICH SHOULD BE SOMEWHERE AROUND...
...HERE!
THERE SHE IS!
HI! I'M PATRICE. THIS IS NATE, AND I APOLOGIZE FOR THAT IN ADVANCE.
LISTEN, HAVE YOU NOTICED ALL THIS MUD? IT'S ONE OF ZOMBOSS' EVIL PLANS. WE NEED YOU TO HELP STOP HIM!
WILL YOU HELP?
IT WOULD BE GREAT IF YOU COULD, BECAUSE, UMM...HEY...
...WHERE'D MY WALLET GO?
Nate Timely's Wallet!
NATE'S COMPLETELY THOUGHT-OUT PIZZA PLAN!
Nate Timely's PIZZA PLAN
1. eat pizza!
INSPIRATIONAL MESSAGE!
EAT PIZZA
1234 5678
Password for Nate
EAT PIZZA
REMINDER LIST OF INTERNET PASSWORDS!
INVISIBLE DUCK
#7
QUACK!
INVISIBLE DUCK #7! FIRST APPEARANCE OF THE SCARLET BREADCRUMB!
SEVEN-FOOT-LONG PIECE OF VOLCANO-FLAVORED TAFFY!

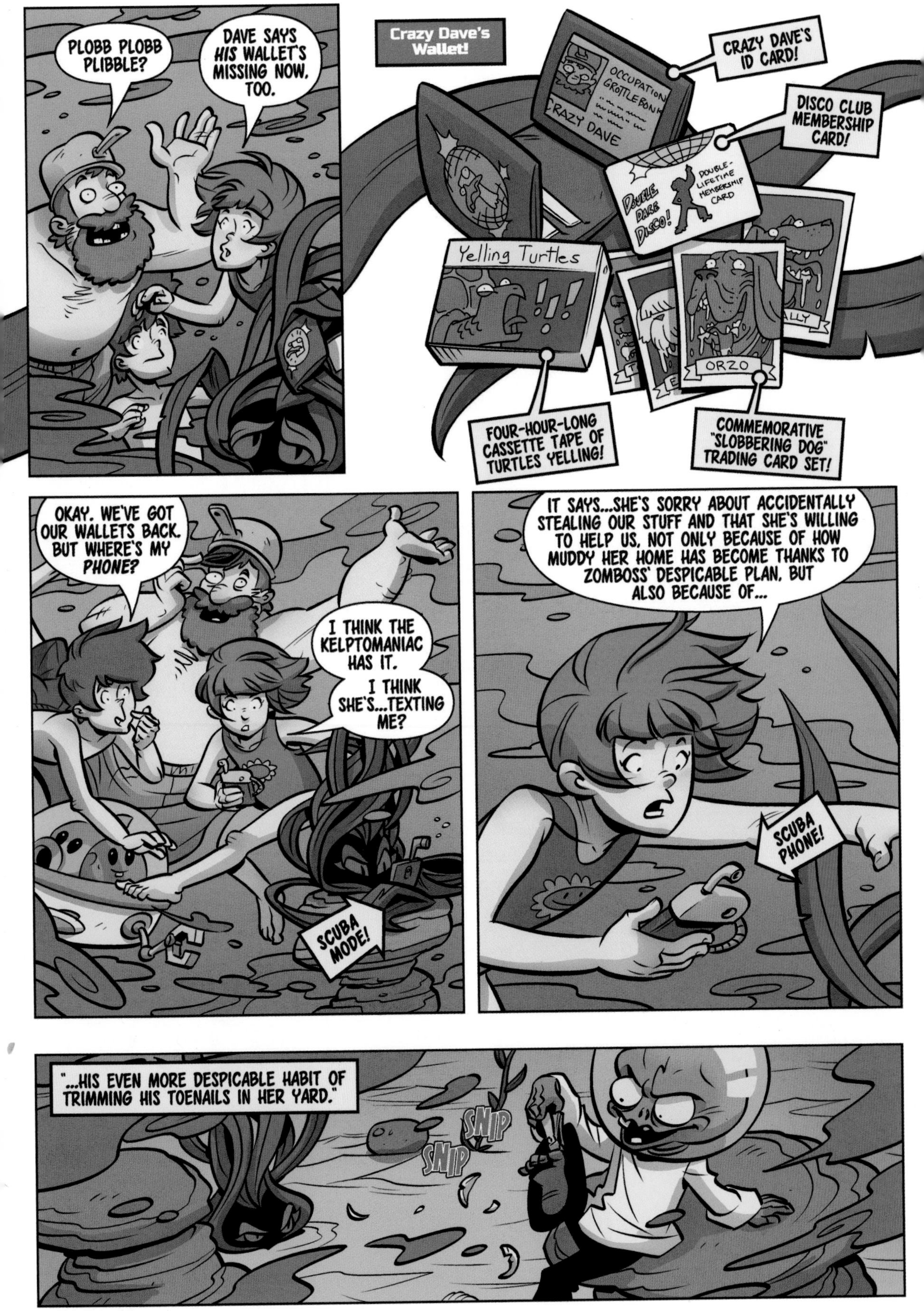
PLOBB PLOBB PLIBBLE?
DAVE SAYS HIS WALLET'S MISSING NOW, TOO.
Crazy Dave's Wallet!
CRAZY DAVE'S ID CARD!
OCCUPATION GROTTLEBONK
CRAZY DAVE
DISCO CLUB MEMBERSHIP CARD!
DOUBLE DARE DISCO!
DOUBLE-LIFETIME MEMBERSHIP CARD
Yelling Turtles
FOUR-HOUR-LONG CASSETTE TAPE OF TURTLES YELLING!
ORZO
COMMEMORATIVE "SLOBBERING DOG" TRADING CARD SET!
OKAY. WE'VE GOT OUR WALLETS BACK. BUT WHERE'S MY PHONE?
I THINK THE KELPTOMANIAC HAS IT.
I THINK SHE'S...TEXTING ME?
SCUBA MODE!
IT SAYS...SHE'S SORRY ABOUT ACCIDENTALLY STEALING OUR STUFF AND THAT SHE'S WILLING TO HELP US, NOT ONLY BECAUSE OF HOW MUDDY HER HOME HAS BECOME THANKS TO ZOMBOSS' DESPICABLE PLAN, BUT ALSO BECAUSE OF...
SCUBA PHONE!
"...HIS EVEN MORE DESPICABLE HABIT OF TRIMMING HIS TOENAILS IN HER YARD."
SNIP
SNIP

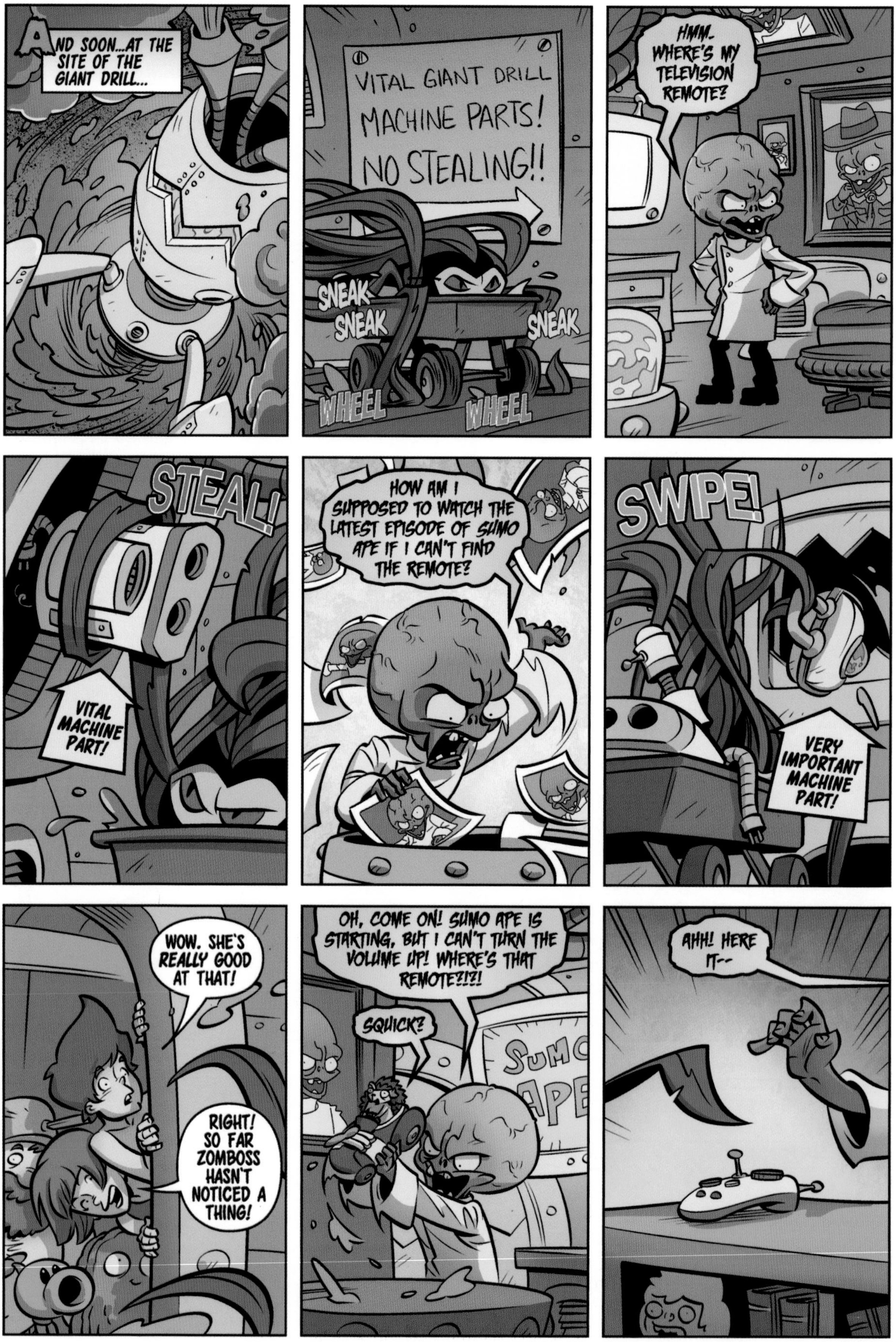
AND SOON...AT THE SITE OF THE GIANT DRILL...
VITAL GIANT DRILL MACHINE PARTS! NO STEALING!!
SNEAK SNEAK
SNEAK
WHEEL
WHEEL
HMM. WHERE'S MY TELEVISION REMOTE?
STEAL!
VITAL MACHINE PART!
HOW AM I SUPPOSED TO WATCH THE LATEST EPISODE OF SUMO APE IF I CAN'T FIND THE REMOTE?
SWIPE!
VERY IMPORTANT MACHINE PART!
WOW. SHE'S REALLY GOOD AT THAT!
RIGHT! SO FAR ZOMBOSS HASN'T NOTICED A THING!
OH, COME ON! SUMO APE IS STARTING, BUT I CAN'T TURN THE VOLUME UP! WHERE'S THAT REMOTE?!?!
SQUICK?
SUMO APE
AHH! HERE IT--

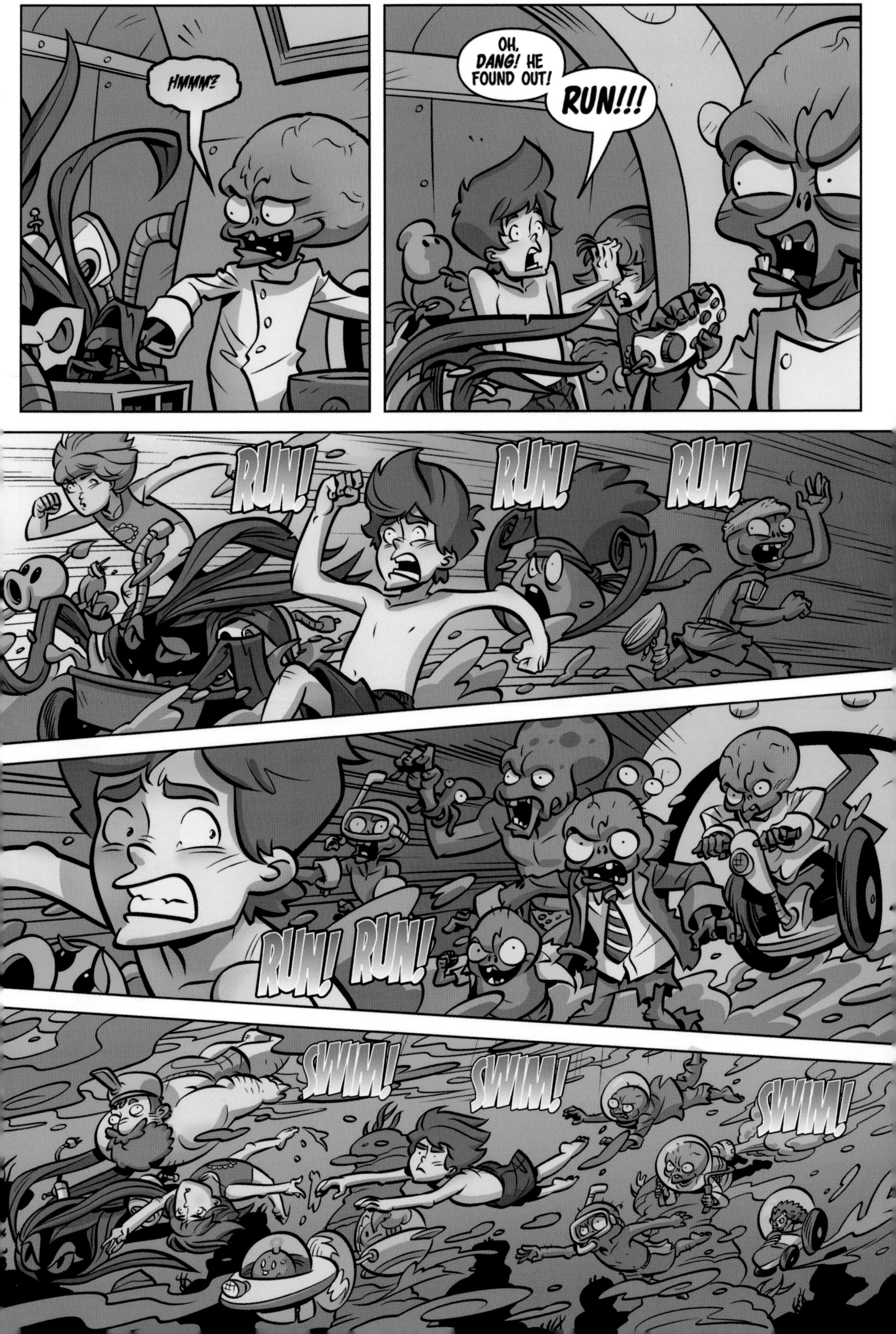
HMMM?
OH, DANG! HE FOUND OUT!
RUN!!!
RUN!
RUN!
RUN!
RUN! RUN!
SWIM!
SWIM!
SWIM!

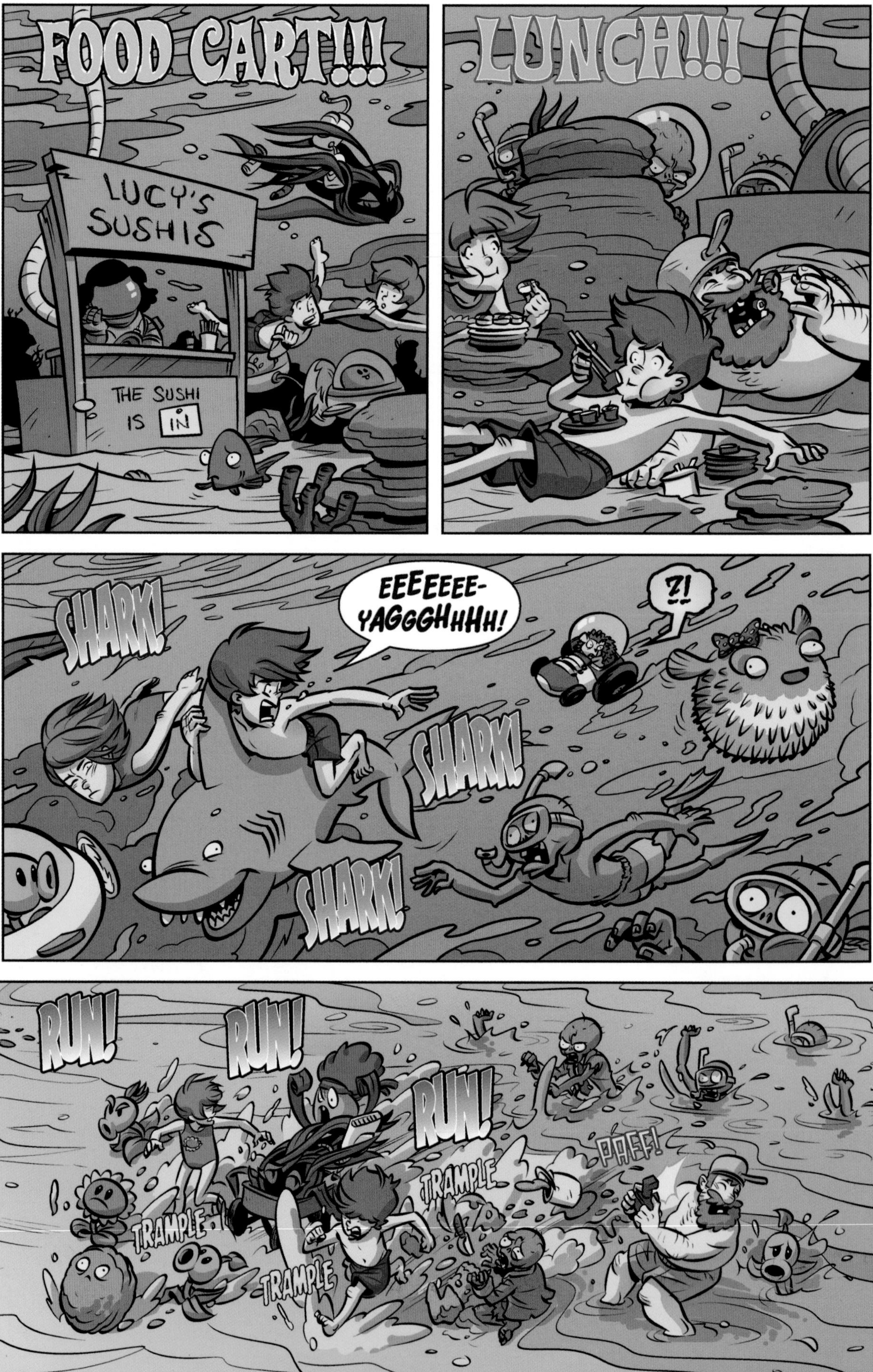
FOOD CART!!!
LUCY'S SUSHIS
THE SUSHI IS IN
LUNCH!!!
SHARK!
EEEEEEE-YAGGGHHHH!
?!
SHARK!
SHARK!
RUN!
RUN!
RUN!
PAFF!
TRAMPLE
TRAMPLE
TRAMPLE

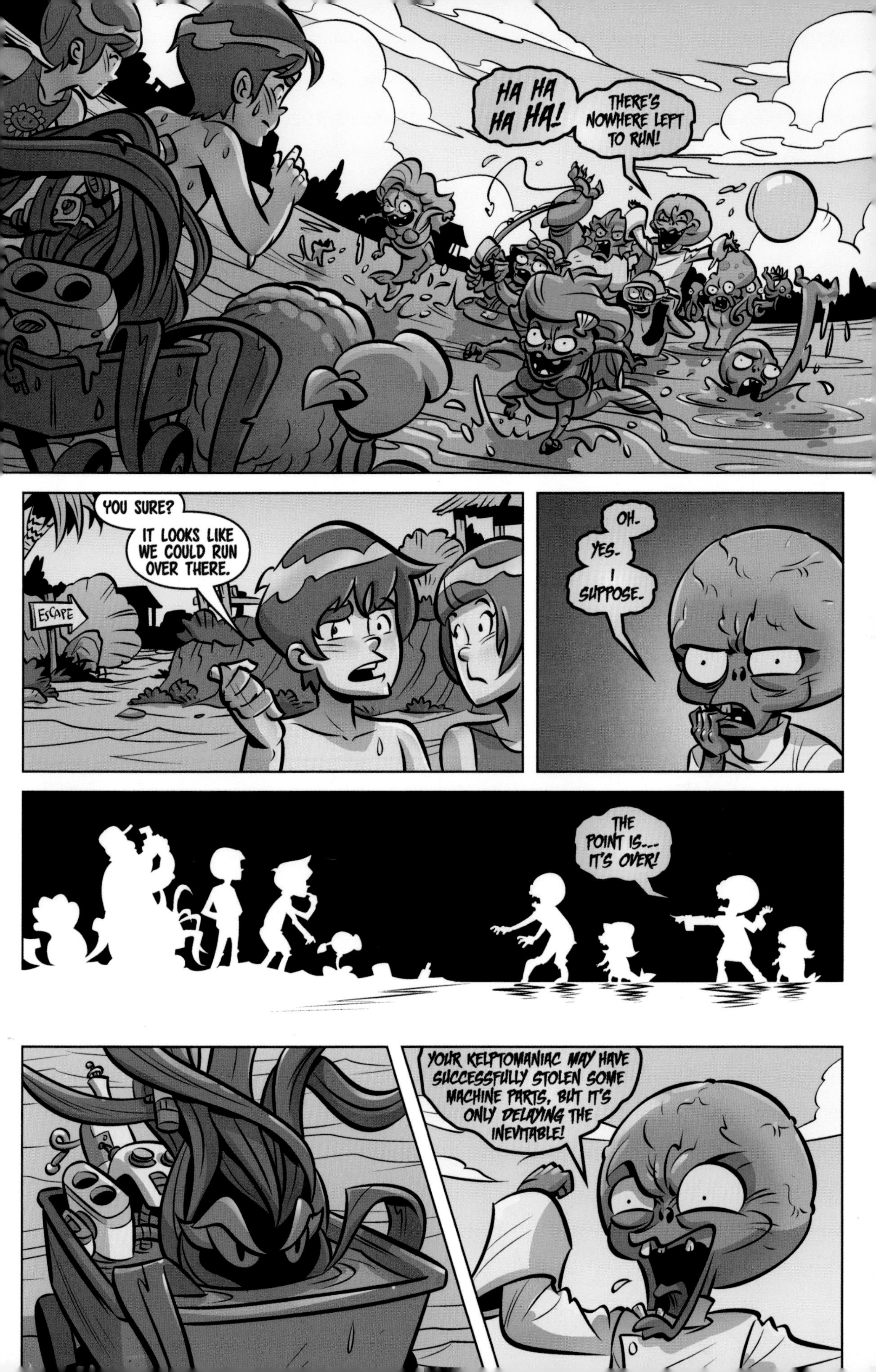
HA HA HA HA!
THERE'S NOWHERE LEFT TO RUN!
YOU SURE?
IT LOOKS LIKE WE COULD RUN OVER THERE.
ESCAPE
OH.
YES.
I SUPPOSE.
THE POINT IS... IT'S OVER!
YOUR KELPTOMANIAC MAY HAVE SUCCESSFULLY STOLEN SOME MACHINE PARTS, BUT IT'S ONLY DELAYING THE INEVITABLE!

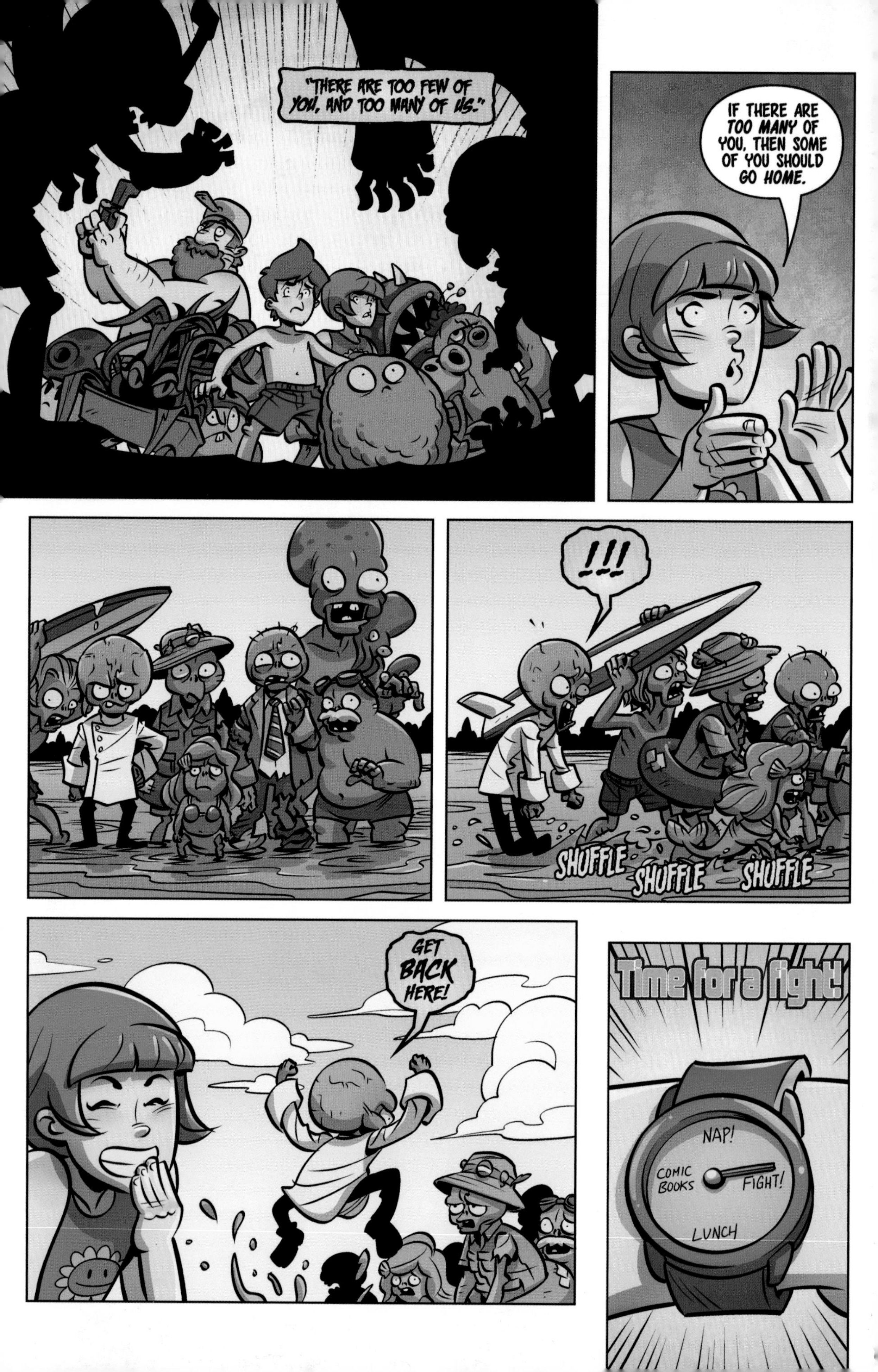
"THERE ARE TOO FEW OF YOU, AND TOO MANY OF US."
IF THERE ARE TOO MANY OF YOU, THEN SOME OF YOU SHOULD GO HOME.
!!!
SHUFFLE
SHUFFLE
SHUFFLE
GET BACK HERE!
Time for a fight!
NAP!
COMIC BOOKS
FIGHT!
LUNCH

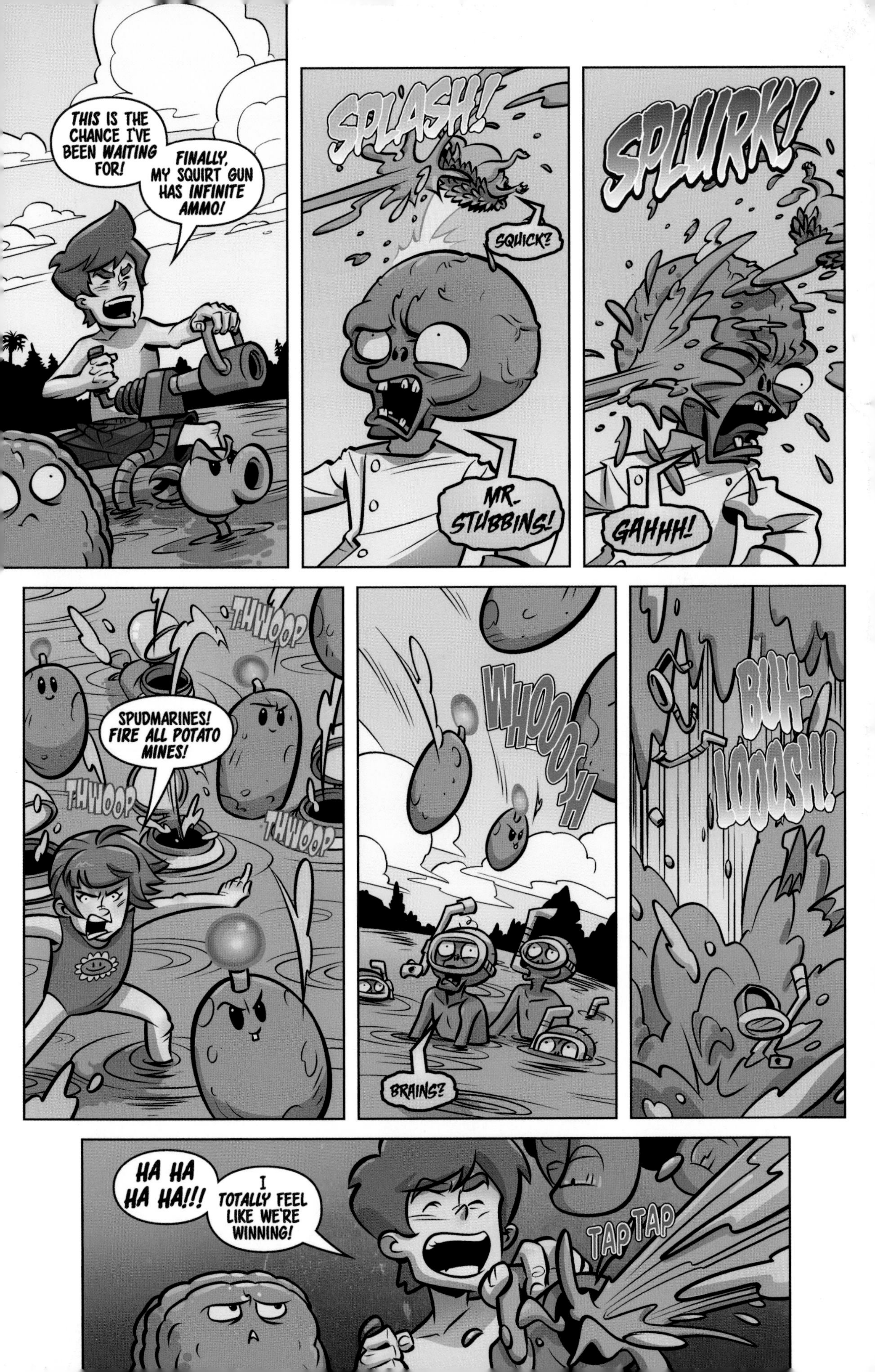
THIS IS THE CHANCE I'VE BEEN WAITING FOR!
FINALLY, MY SQUIRT GUN HAS INFINITE AMMO!
SPLASH!
SQUICK?
MR. STUBBINS!
SPLURK!
GAHHH!
THWOOP
SPUDMARINES! FIRE ALL POTATO MINES!
THWOOP
THWOOP
WHOOOOSH
BRAINS?
BUH-LOOOSH!
HA HA HA HA!!!
I TOTALLY FEEL LIKE WE'RE WINNING!
TAP TAP

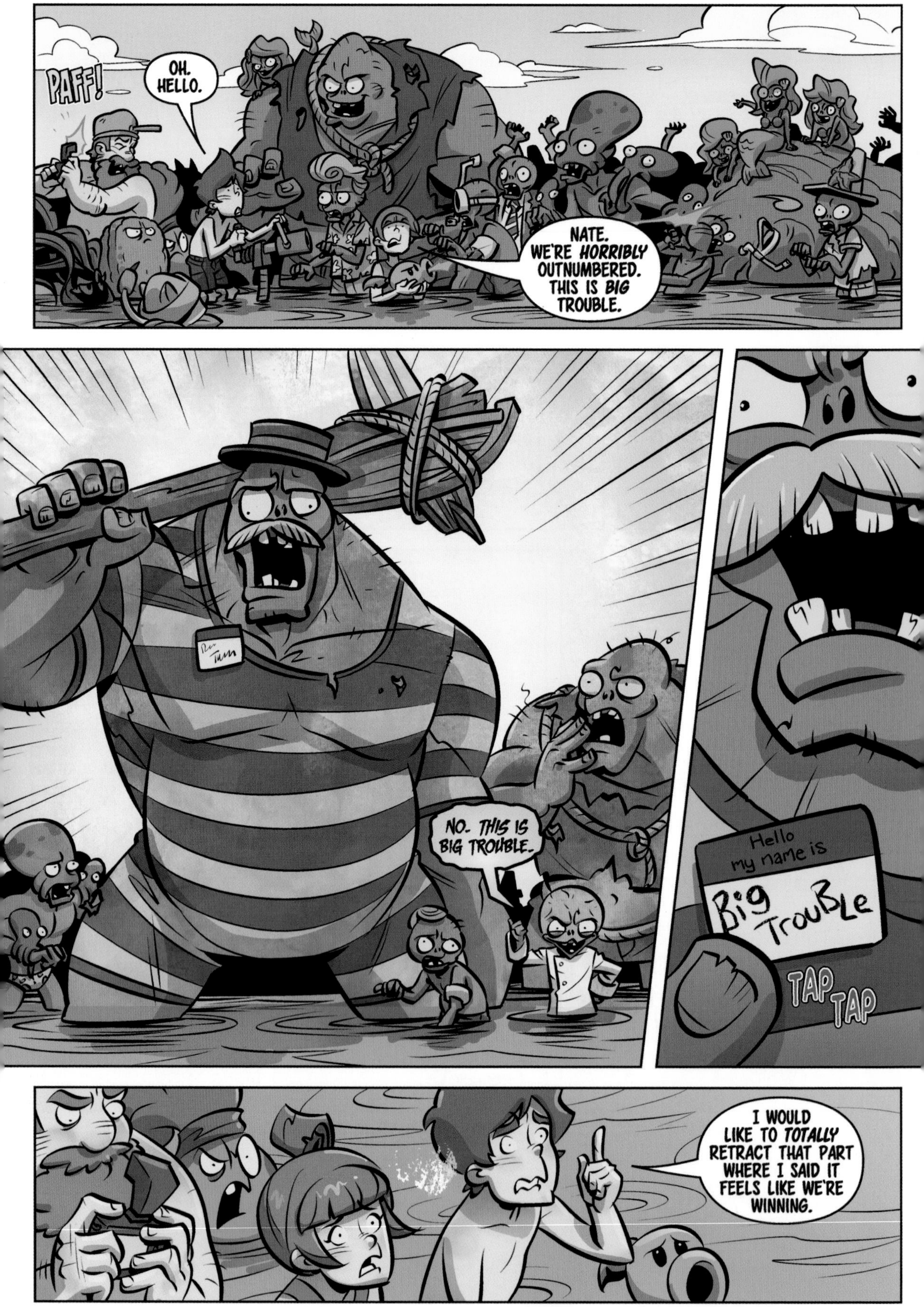
PAFF!
OH. HELLO.
NATE. WE'RE HORRIBLY OUTNUMBERED. THIS IS BIG TROUBLE.
NO. THIS IS BIG TROUBLE.
Hello my name is
Big TrouBLe
TAP TAP
I WOULD LIKE TO TOTALLY RETRACT THAT PART WHERE I SAID IT FEELS LIKE WE'RE WINNING.

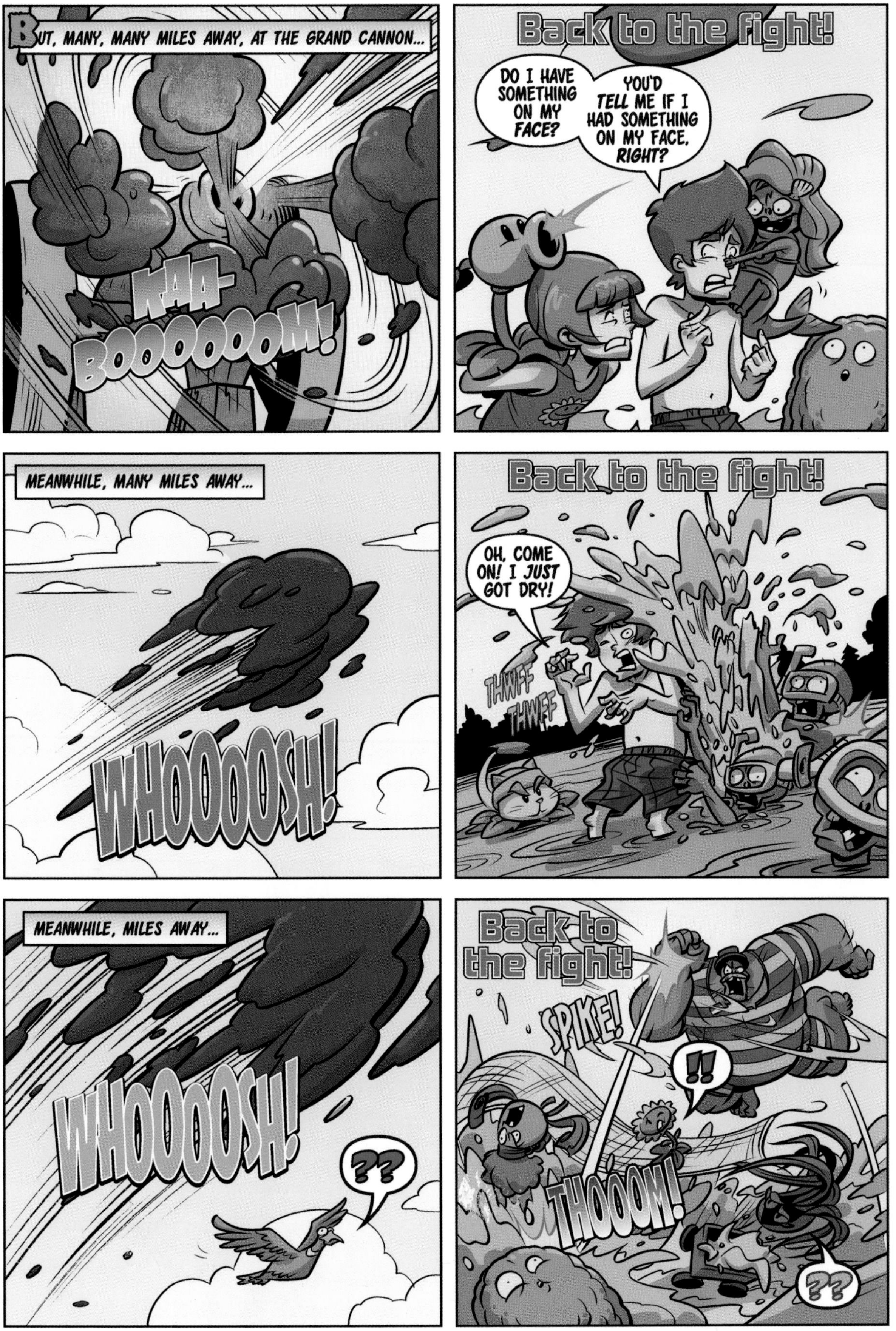
BUT, MANY, MANY MILES AWAY, AT THE GRAND CANNON...
KAA-BOOOOOOOM!
Back to the fight!
DO I HAVE SOMETHING ON MY FACE?
YOU'D TELL ME IF I HAD SOMETHING ON MY FACE, RIGHT?
MEANWHILE, MANY MILES AWAY...
WHOOOOSH!
Back to the fight!
OH, COME ON! I JUST GOT DRY!
THWFF THWFF
MEANWHILE, MILES AWAY...
WHOOOOSH!
??
Back to the fight!
SPIKE!
!!
THOOOM!
??

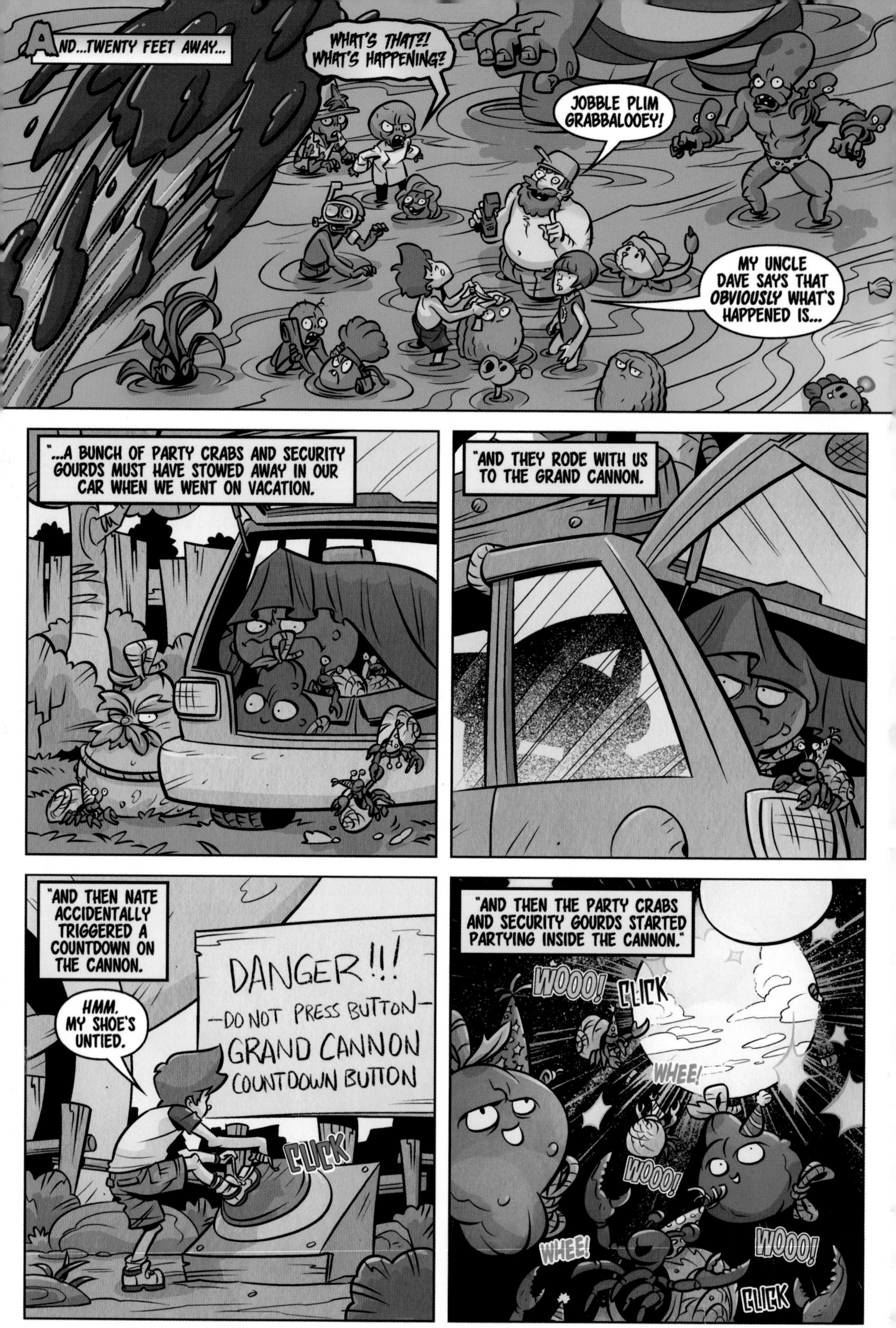
AND...TWENTY FEET AWAY...
WHAT'S THAT?! WHAT'S HAPPENING?
JOBBLE PLIM GRABBALOOEY!
MY UNCLE DAVE SAYS THAT OBVIOUSLY WHAT'S HAPPENED IS...
"...A BUNCH OF PARTY CRABS AND SECURITY GOURDS MUST HAVE STOWED AWAY IN OUR CAR WHEN WE WENT ON VACATION.
"AND THEY RODE WITH US TO THE GRAND CANNON.
"AND THEN NATE ACCIDENTALLY TRIGGERED A COUNTDOWN ON THE CANNON.
HMM. MY SHOE'S UNTIED.
DANGER!!!
—DO NOT PRESS BUTTON—
GRAND CANNON
COUNTDOWN BUTTON
CLICK
"AND THEN THE PARTY CRABS AND SECURITY GOURDS STARTED PARTYING INSIDE THE CANNON."
WOOO!
CLICK
WHEE!
WOOO!
WHEE!
WOOO!
CLICK

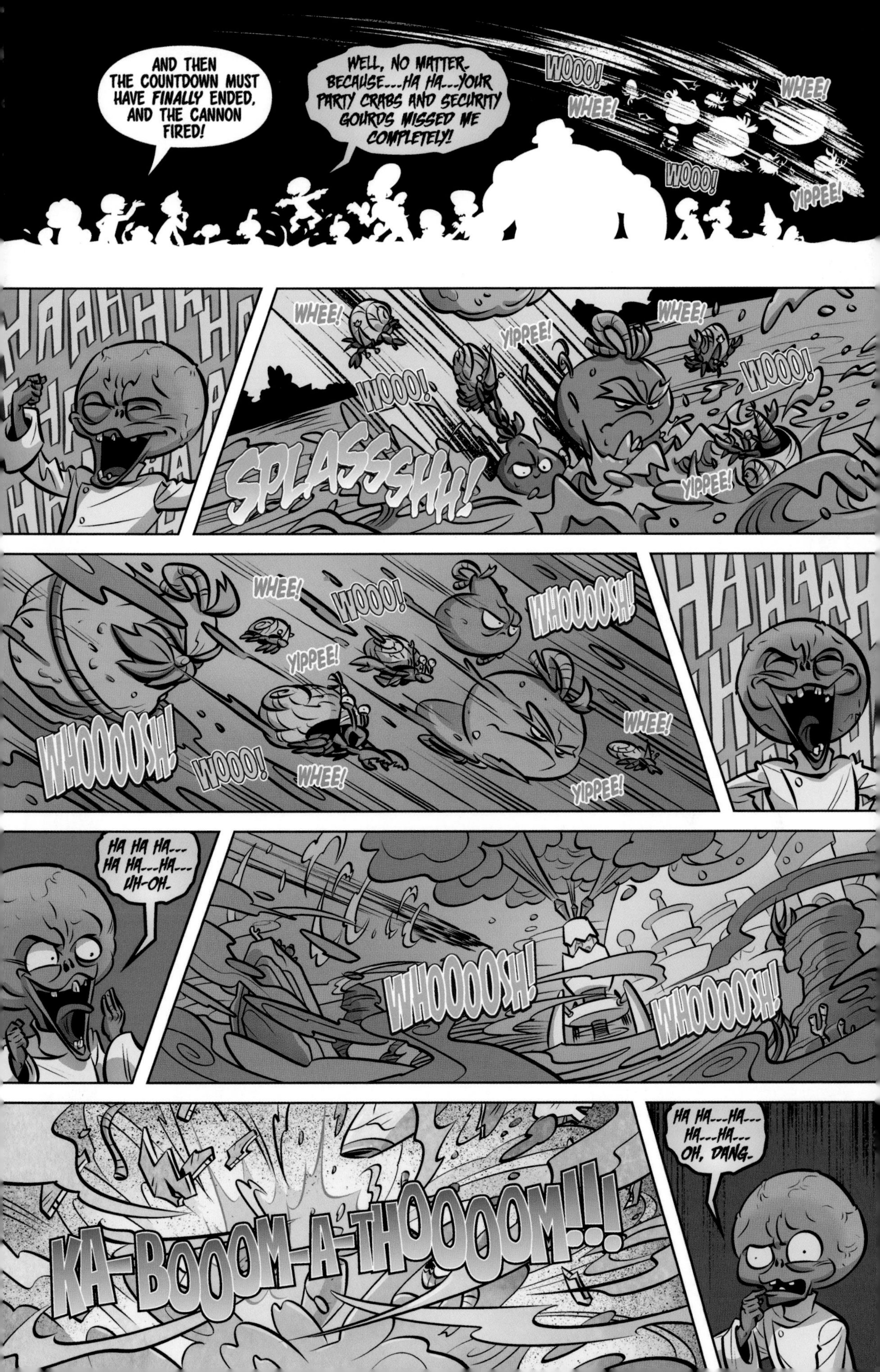
AND THEN THE COUNTDOWN MUST HAVE FINALLY ENDED, AND THE CANNON FIRED!
WELL, NO MATTER. BECAUSE...HA HA...YOUR PARTY CRABS AND SECURITY GOURDS MISSED ME COMPLETELY!
WOOO!
WHEE!
WHEE!
WOOO!
YIPPEE!
WHEE!
YIPPEE!
WHEE!
WOOO!
WOOO!
SPLASSSHH!
YIPPEE!
WHEE!
WOOO!
WHOOOOSH!
YIPPEE!
WHOOOOSH!
WOOO!
WHEE!
WHEE!
YIPPEE!
HA HA HA... HA HA...HA... UH-OH.
WHOOOOSH!
WHOOOOSH!
KA-BOOOM-A-THOOOOM!!!
HA HA...HA... HA...HA... OH, DANG.

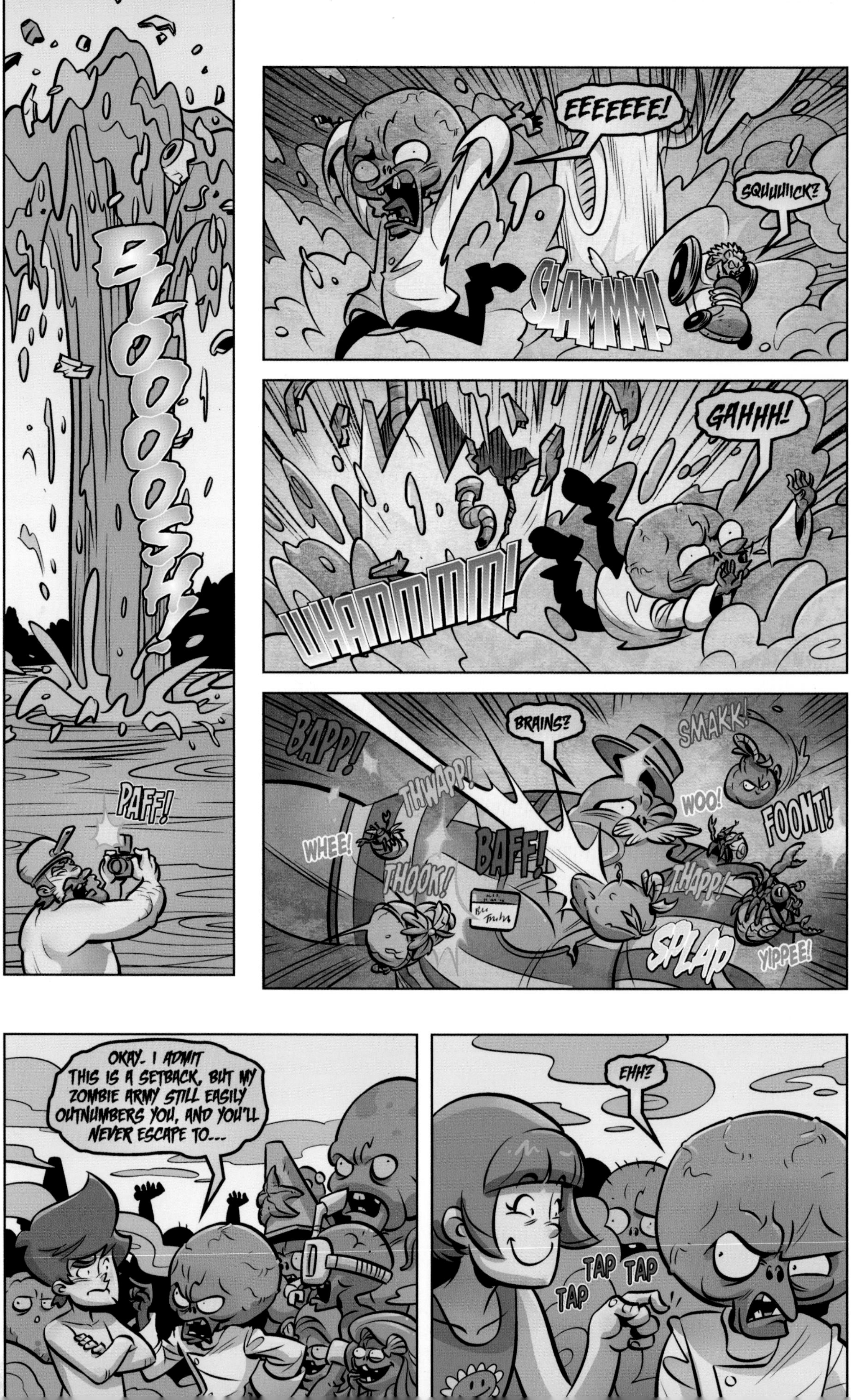
BLOOOOOSH!
PAFF!
EEEEEEE!
SQUUUIICK?
SLAMMM!
GAHHH!
WHAMMMM!
BAPP!
BRAINS?
SMAKK!
THWAPP!
WOO!
FOONT!
WHEE!
BAFF!
THOOK!
THAPP!
SPLAP
YIPPEE!
OKAY. I ADMIT THIS IS A SETBACK, BUT MY ZOMBIE ARMY STILL EASILY OUTNUMBERS YOU, AND YOU'LL NEVER ESCAPE TO...
EHH?
TAP TAP TAP

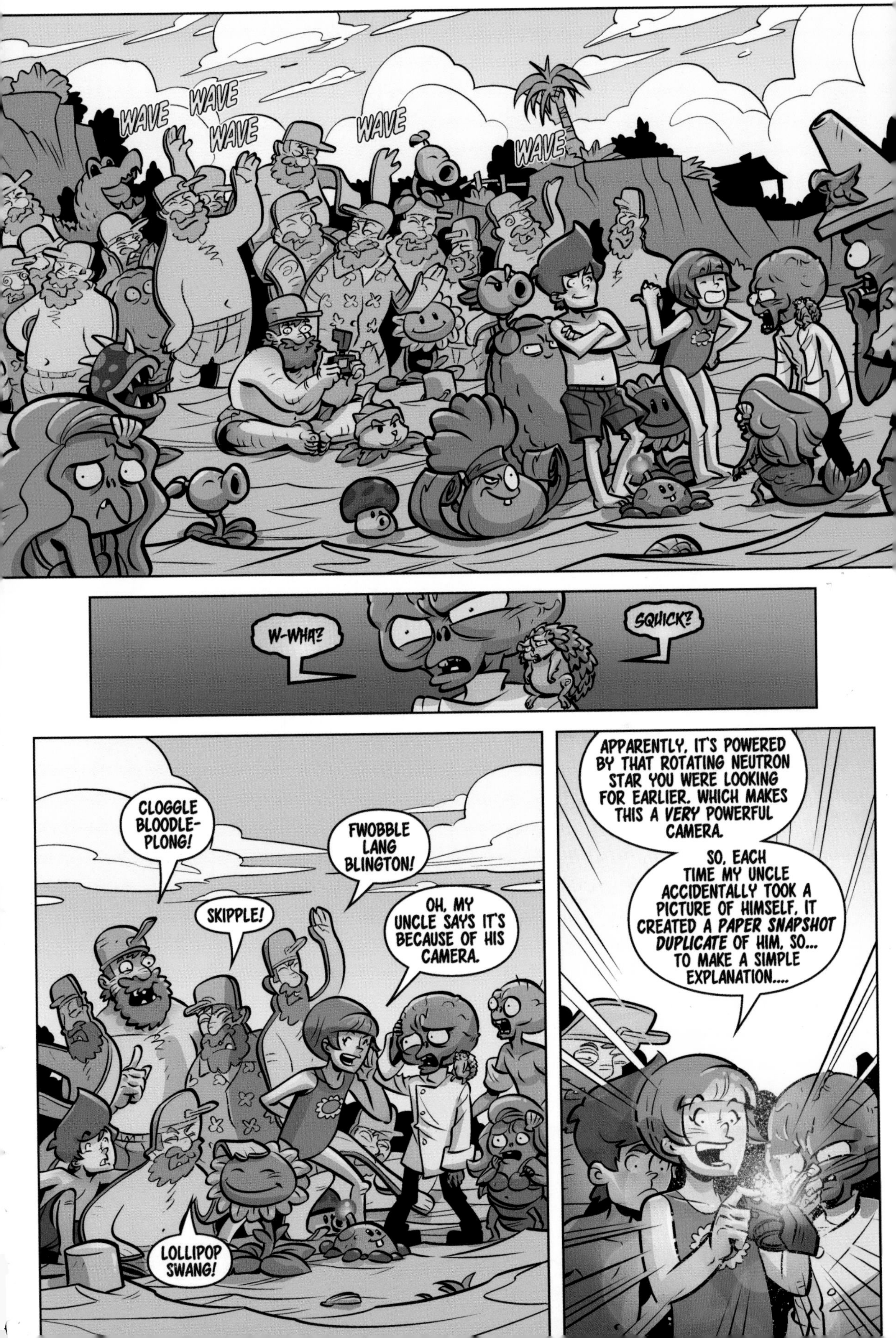
WAVE
WAVE
WAVE
WAVE
WAVE
W-WHA?
SQUICK?
CLOGGLE BLOODLE-PLONG!
FWOBBLE LANG BLINGTON!
SKIPPLE!
OH, MY UNCLE SAYS IT'S BECAUSE OF HIS CAMERA.
LOLLIPOP SWANG!
APPARENTLY, IT'S POWERED BY THAT ROTATING NEUTRON STAR YOU WERE LOOKING FOR EARLIER. WHICH MAKES THIS A VERY POWERFUL CAMERA.
SO, EACH TIME MY UNCLE ACCIDENTALLY TOOK A PICTURE OF HIMSELF, IT CREATED A PAPER SNAPSHOT DUPLICATE OF HIM, SO... TO MAKE A SIMPLE EXPLANATION....

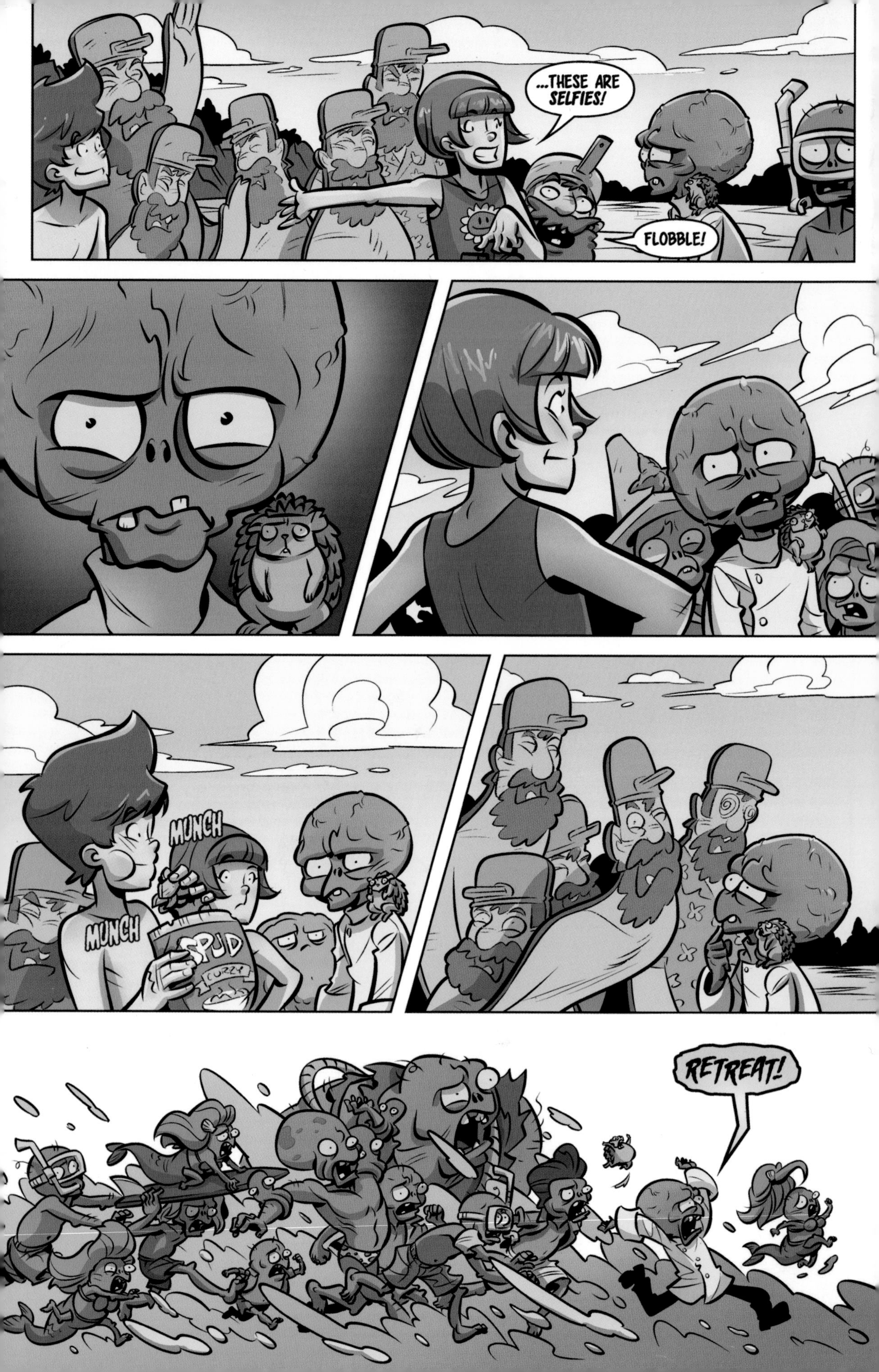
...THESE ARE SELFIES!
FLOBBLE!
MUNCH
MUNCH
SPUD
RETREAT!

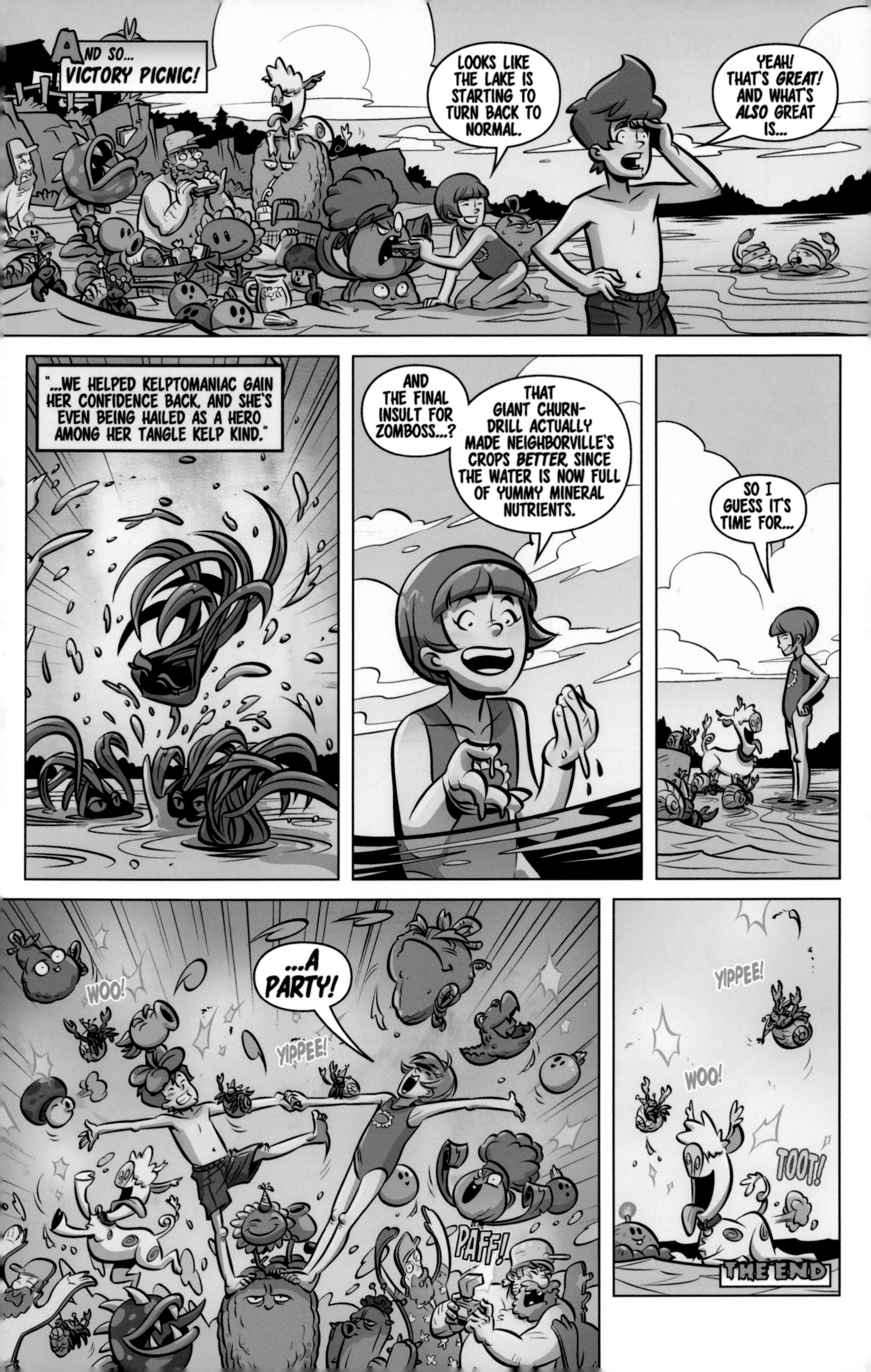
AND SO... VICTORY PICNIC!
LOOKS LIKE THE LAKE IS STARTING TO TURN BACK TO NORMAL.
YEAH! THAT'S GREAT! AND WHAT'S ALSO GREAT IS...
"...WE HELPED KELPTOMANIAC GAIN HER CONFIDENCE BACK, AND SHE'S EVEN BEING HAILED AS A HERO AMONG HER TANGLE KELP KIND."
AND THE FINAL INSULT FOR ZOMBOSS...?
THAT GIANT CHURN-DRILL ACTUALLY MADE NEIGHBORVILLE'S CROPS BETTER, SINCE THE WATER IS NOW FULL OF YUMMY MINERAL NUTRIENTS.
SO I GUESS IT'S TIME FOR...
...A PARTY!
WOO!
YIPPEE!
PAFF!
YIPPEE!
WOO!
TOOT!
THE END

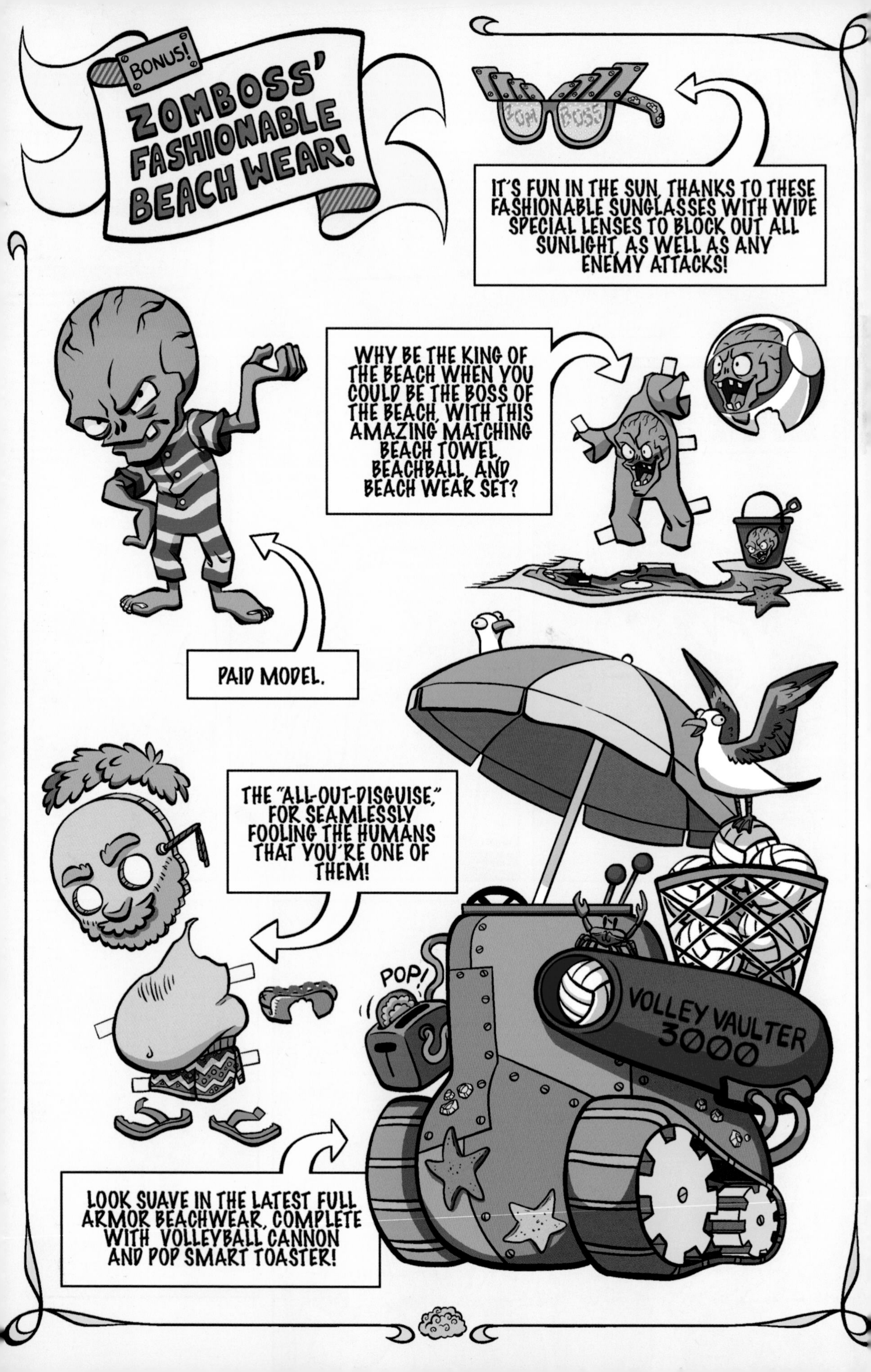
BONUS!
ZOMBOSS' FASHIONABLE BEACH WEAR!
ZOM BOSS
IT'S FUN IN THE SUN, THANKS TO THESE FASHIONABLE SUNGLASSES WITH WIDE SPECIAL LENSES TO BLOCK OUT ALL SUNLIGHT, AS WELL AS ANY ENEMY ATTACKS!
WHY BE THE KING OF THE BEACH WHEN YOU COULD BE THE BOSS OF THE BEACH, WITH THIS AMAZING MATCHING BEACH TOWEL, BEACHBALL, AND BEACH WEAR SET?
PAID MODEL.
THE "ALL-OUT-DISGUISE," FOR SEAMLESSLY FOOLING THE HUMANS THAT YOU'RE ONE OF THEM!
POP!
VOLLEY VAULTER 3000
LOOK SUAVE IN THE LATEST FULL ARMOR BEACHWEAR, COMPLETE WITH VOLLEYBALL CANNON AND POP SMART TOASTER!

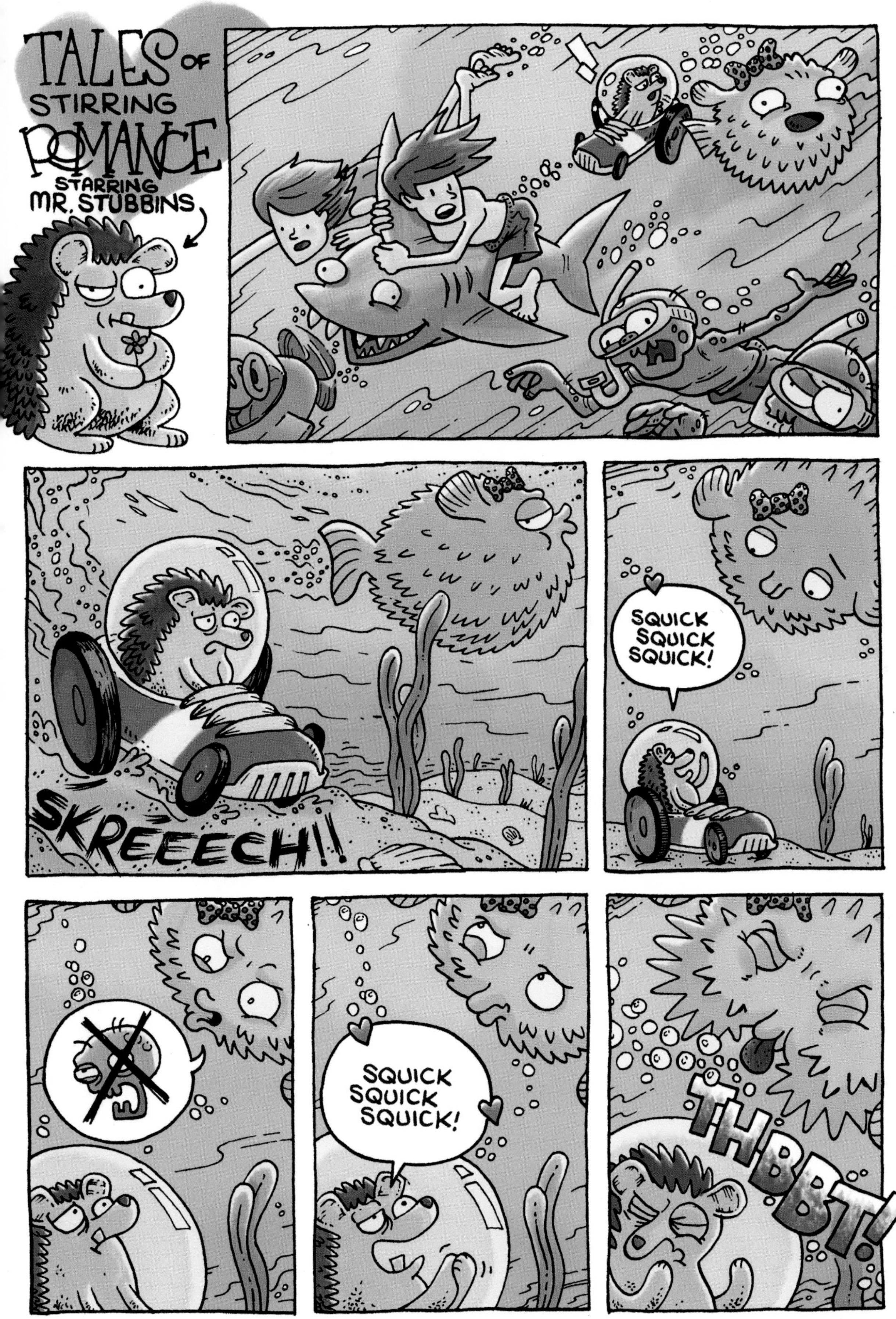
TALES OF STIRRING ROMANCE
STARRING MR. STUBBINS
SKREEECH!!
SQUICK SQUICK SQUICK!
SQUICK SQUICK SQUICK!
THBBT!

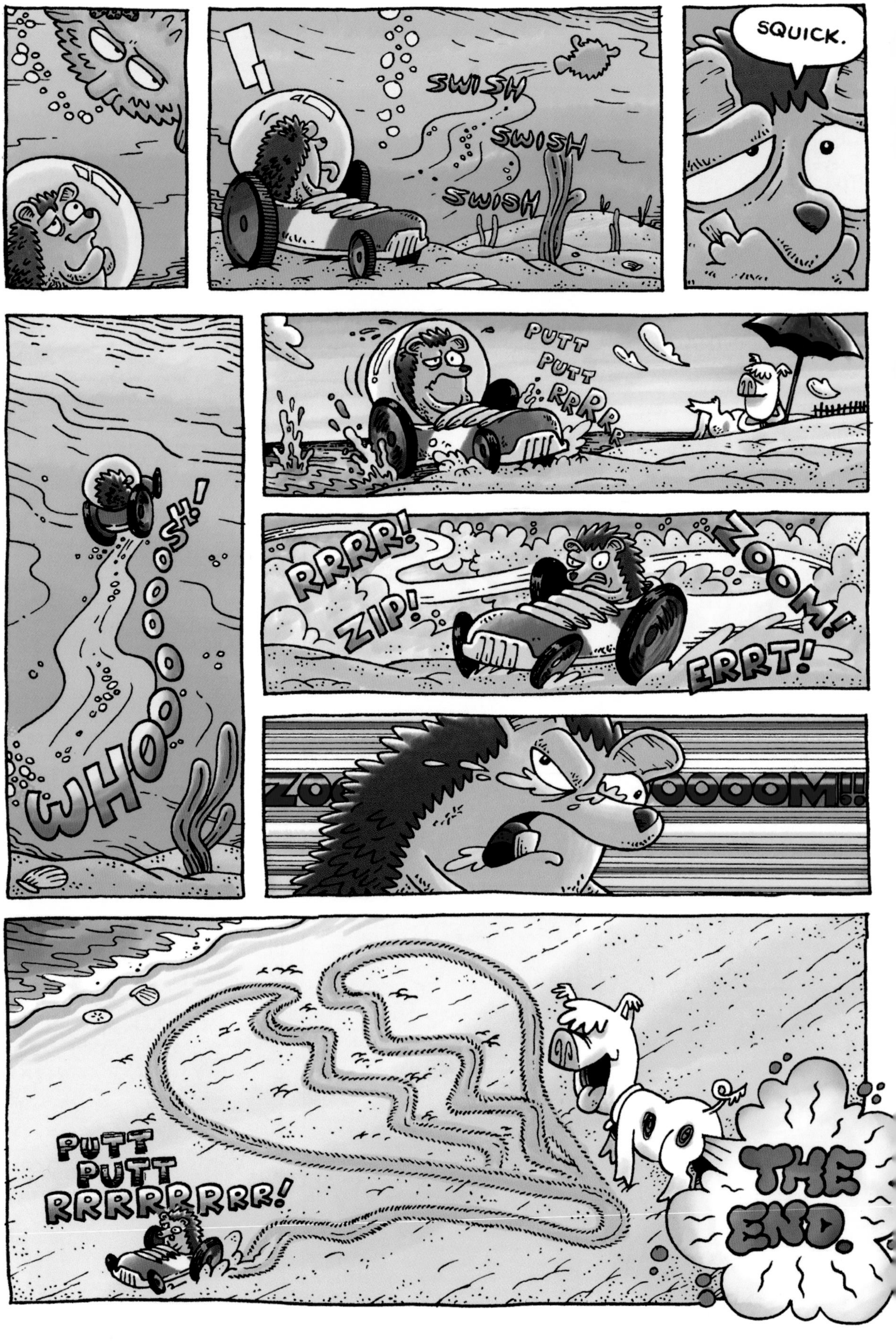
SWISH
SWISH
SWISH
SQUICK.
WHOOOOOOOSH!
PUTT
PUTT
RRRRRR
RRRR!
ZIP!
ZOOM!
ERRT!
ZOO OOOOM!!
PUTT
PUTT
RRRRRRRR!
THE END.